THE BODY AT THE WINDMILL

KATE HARDY

Storm

Ebook ISBN: 978-1-83700-272-6
Paperback ISBN: 978-1-83700-274-0

Cover design by: Lisa Brewster
Cover images by: Shutterstock

Published by Storm Publishing.
For further information, visit:
www.stormpublishing.co

A Georgina Drake Mystery

The Body at Rookery Barn

The Body in the Ice House

The Body Under the Stage

The Body in the Lighthouse

The Body at the Roman Baths

The Body at the Vineyard

For Gerard – thank you for always indulging me

ONE

'I'm really sorry, Georgie,' Jodie said, ending the call. 'That was the school. Harry's feeling sick and I need to pick him up from Great Wenborough Windmill.'

'Poor boy,' Georgie said. 'I know you said he was on a school trip today, but I didn't realise it was at the windmill.'

'They're doing Victorian studies this term,' Jodie explained. 'Louise Wilkins, who restored the windmill at Great Wenborough, runs education days to show the kids how grain used to be milled back in the old days and turned into flour.'

'What a shame he's going to miss out,' Georgina said. 'And I'm sorry he's poorly.'

'Yeah.' Jodie bit her lip. 'I'll ring my brother and see if he can give us a lift.'

'Don't worry. I'll take you,' Georgina said, knowing that Jodie's car was in the local garage having a problem fixed and her brother, Mike, the landlord of the Red Lion, had dropped her off at Rookery Farm this morning.

'I can't ask you—' Jodie began.

'You're not asking. I'm offering,' Georgina cut in gently. 'Let's go and get Harry. I'll grab a towel and a plastic bag in case he feels ill on the way home.'

'Thank you,' Jodie said gratefully. 'If Mum can come to my place and sit with him, I'll come back and finish cleaning the barn with you.' Rookery Barn was a former dairy at Georgina's home, which she let out as a holiday cottage. Jodie helped to get it ready on Fridays, which was changeover day. Today was Monday; as nobody was staying at the cottage that week, Jodie was helping Georgina with a deep clean.

Georgina smiled at the younger woman. 'Don't worry. I'll manage,' she said. 'And I'll still be paying you for today. Harry needs to come first, and if he's feeling ill, he'll want you with him.' She settled Bert, her liver-and-white English springer spaniel, into his bed in the farmhouse kitchen, and they set off for Great Wenborough. It was only a matter of minutes before Georgina parked outside the windmill in the next village. She and Jodie went to the white-painted stable door of the five-storey windmill, where twenty-five children, a teacher and a couple of anxious-looking parent helpers were waiting.

'Quite a lot of the children are feeling ill and I've had to get them all picked up. There seems to be a nasty bug doing the rounds,' Miss Hurst, the temporary teacher of Harry's Year Four class, told them. Georgina noticed that the teacher's face had a pale, almost green cast; it looked as if the poor woman was coming down with the same bug as the children and was doing her best to resist it until all her charges were safely collected.

'All right, Harry, your mum's here and you can go.' Miss Hurst ticked him off a list.

'My tummy hurts, Mum,' Harry said as they got to the car. 'And I feel sick. Robbie' – one of his best friends, who'd been involved with a case Colin had investigated at the lighthouse in Summerstrand, the previous year – 'was really sick. It went all over his shoes. And it was *green*.'

'All right. Well, we've got a plastic bag,' Jodie said. 'Sit with it on your lap.' Once he'd climbed into the back of the car, she tucked a towel over him, shook the plastic bag open, and handed it to him.

'Use the bag if you think you're going to be sick,' she said as she sat beside him.

'Though it doesn't matter if you miss,' Georgina added. 'It's easily cleaned up. You're more important, Harry.'

'Thank you, Georgie.' His usually cheerful face was miserable, and he wasn't chatting as much as he normally did.

'Open a window, Jodie. The fresh air might help a bit,' Georgina suggested. 'Sorry you're feeling poorly, Harry. And it's such a shame that the whole class seems to have gone down with the bug at the same time. You've all missed out on what sounded like a really fun trip.'

'Thank you for coming to get me,' Harry said politely.

Georgina smiled, knowing that Jodie was strict about manners – and it made Harry all the nicer to be around. When Jodie occasionally asked her to babysit, Georgina was always happy to agree. 'No problem, sweetheart.'

'There was a dead rat,' he pronounced next. Except there was none of the glee in his delivery that you'd usually expect from a nine-year-old boy.

'Where?' Jodie asked, sounding shocked.

'In the grain store. It was all stiff, stretched out right in front of the sacks of wheat.' He paused. 'Miss Hurst screamed.'

'Well, a dead rat isn't the sort of thing you expect to see.' Jodie shuddered. 'I hate to think it might've been eating the wheat that was turned into fl—'

The rest of her words were lost in the sound of Harry being sick into the plastic bag.

'Sorry,' he said miserably when the bout of vomiting was over.

'It's all right,' Georgina reassured him. 'Don't worry. We'll get you home, love, and your mum can sort you out.'

Getting rid of the contents of his stomach had clearly helped, because Harry sounded chirpier when he continued his story. 'Mrs Wilkins, who owns the mill, screamed when she saw the rat, too. So did Sam's gran. But Annie-the-nanny didn't.'

'Who's Annie-the-nanny?' Georgina asked.

'Annie Newman,' Jodie explained. 'She's Louise's nanny. Louise's oldest son, Sam, is in Harry's class. Sam's brother, Noah, is in Year One and Isla, their baby sister, is at the preschool.'

'Sam doesn't like Annie. He says she's mean,' Harry confided. 'His gran is his dad's mum. Sam likes her. She normally lives in London, but something went wrong in her flat and she had to come and live with them a couple of months ago until the builders sort it out. They've moved Sam's bed into the dining room for her, because she's got a bad knee and can't manage to get up the stairs, and Sam's sleeping on a camp bed until she goes back to London. His gran buys him lots of sweets and he always shares them with us.'

If Harry was chatting, he was definitely on the mend, Georgina thought with a smile. And that was worth putting up with the unpleasant sour smell emanating from his temporary sick bag.

'I have to admit, I don't like Annie Newman very much, either – though don't you dare tell anyone I said that, Harry,' Jodie warned.

'Why not?' Georgina asked.

'She's a bit cold and she doesn't chat at the school gates with the rest of us,' Jodie said. 'Louise picks the kids up on Wednesdays, when the bakery's closed for a half day, and she's lovely – she mixes with the mums properly.'

'Sam's mum and his gran gave us all chicken sausage rolls when we got there this morning,' Harry said. 'They were delicious. And they were still war—' The rest of the sentence was cut off by another bout of vomiting.

'Sorry,' he mumbled again when it had finished.

'No need to apologise, love,' Georgina said. 'It's not your fault you're unwell.'

Once she'd dropped Jodie and Harry off, she opened all the windows of the car to let fresh air blow out the smell of puke as she drove home. January was the peak season for the winter vomiting virus, she knew; though it did seem a bit odd that the whole class and the teacher appeared to have gone down with it at the same time, and they'd all been so severely affected.

All the same, she decided to cancel coffee with her friend Sybbie Walters that afternoon. Although viruses tended to spread via close contact and Georgina planned to put on a mask and gloves before she cleaned the back of the car, she didn't want to risk picking up the virus and passing it on to Sybbie – or, even worse, to Sybbie's five-week-old granddaughter, Elizabeth. When she arrived back at Rookery Farm, Georgina parked in her usual place on the gravelled area by the kitchen door and left the car doors open to help air it out, before sitting at her kitchen table and ringing Sybbie.

'Given that the whole class seems to have gone down with it at the same time,' Georgina said after she'd explained what had happened, 'it's obviously quite a virulent strain. I'll probably know by tomorrow if I've caught the bug, too. But in the meantime I'd rather not risk passing on anything nasty to you or to Lizzie.'

'That's a shame. Cesca and I were really looking forward to seeing you,' Sybbie said.

Just as Georgina had been looking forward to seeing them. 'Give the baby a cuddle for me. As soon as I know I'm clear of the virus, maybe we can reschedule?' she asked hopefully.

'Of course, dear girl,' Sybbie said. 'Though it's an odd type of virus that wipes out a whole class all at once – and so quickly, too.'

So Georgina wasn't the only one who thought it was suspicious. Then again, given that her partner, Colin, was a detective, Georgina wondered whether maybe she was overthinking things. 'Maybe it's been brewing for a day or so. And I guess warm sausage rolls are the worst thing to eat when you're feeling a bit rough – that might be why they were all complaining of a stomachache and throwing up. Once someone starts being sick, the sound and smell tends to make everyone else feel sick, too, doesn't it?' Georgina said. 'I felt for the poor teacher. She looked pretty green, herself. But obviously she couldn't leave the windmill until all the kids had been picked up.'

'Great Wenborough Mill, you said?' Sybbie asked. 'That's Louise Wilkins's place. She supplies the farm shop with fresh yeast and locally-ground flour, and also she's supplying some of our bread during Cesca's maternity leave. I was hoping to have a nosey round the mill at some point. Louise spent a year restoring it, and she's got it set up just as it used to be in the 1870s – all five floors of it. It must be fascinating, seeing the whole process from a sack of grain being hoisted to the top of the mill, then tipped into the hoppers and turned into flour, and then the flour going straight into the bakery and being made into bread.'

'I wouldn't mind seeing that, too,' Georgina said. 'You know, that might make a really interesting feature for the local press.'

Sybbie chuckled. 'And you'll find the interesting angles for the photographs. Maybe Cesca can come, too, and Bernard can babysit Lizzie.'

'Not forgetting Jodie,' Georgina said, 'so the whole gang can enjoy it.' Over the past couple of years, they'd all been involved in helping to solve some of Colin's cases and the cold cases that had occurred alongside, and the four of them had become a tightly knit team. 'And then we can have a cup of tea and a sausage roll in the bakery café afterwards.'

'Great idea,' Sybbie said.

TWO

The next morning, Jodie called Georgina, sounding worried. 'Harry's feeling a lot better today,' she said. 'So are all the other kids in his class, though everyone on the class's group chat reckons we should keep the kids off for another day or two, to make sure everyone's clear of the bugs.'

'That's a good idea – but it's even better news that Harry's fine,' Georgina said.

'Yes, but there's some really terrible news from school,' Jodie continued. 'Miss Hurst, the teacher who is covering Mrs James's maternity leave, died last night.'

'What, from the bug?' Georgina asked, shocked.

'Apparently there's going to be a post-mortem,' Jodie said. 'She didn't have anything wrong with her – at least, nothing anyone knows of – and all the kids are fine now. So why did she die?'

'A post-mortem's quite usual in cases of unexpected deaths,' Georgina reassured her. 'Poor woman. And her poor family. How awful for them.'

'It just seems a bit – well, weird,' Jodie said. 'A whole class being ill, all at the same time, and then their teacher dying. There was that dead rat, too, and we all know rats spread disease. I don't mean the bubonic plague from their fleas, either,' she added. 'It's why we're not meant to swim in rivers – in case we pick up Weil's disease from rat pee.'

Georgina knew that cases of the bubonic plague were still reported across the world, every so often. She'd read an article about a wildlife biologist contracting the disease and sadly dying from it after examining the dead body of a mountain lion. 'Even the bubonic plague can be cured now, given the right antibiotics,' she said, but her friend had a point. It was a bit too much of a coincidence. Colin always muttered that he didn't believe in coincidences. 'Anyway, I'm glad Harry's better.' She paused. 'What about the parent helpers yesterday?'

'They're absolutely fine,' Jodie said.

And that was odd, too. Why would Louise and two of the adults not go down with the bug, while Miss Hurst had died and all the children had been ill? Or maybe she was overthinking it again. 'Try not to worry,' Georgina added.

When she spoke to Sybbie on the phone, a few minutes later, her friend was also pleased to hear that Harry was on the mend, but shocked to hear the news about the class's temporary teacher. 'The poor woman had only been at the school for a week, covering Melanie James's maternity leave,' Sybbie said. 'How terrible for her family.'

'Isn't it just?' Georgina asked. 'I feel sorry for Louise Wilkins, too. Everyone's going to be pointing a finger at her now – especially as there was a dead rat in the grain store when she was showing the children round.'

'A dead *rat*?' Sybbie asked. 'Hmm.'

'What's the "hmm" for?' Georgina asked.

'I recommended the local pest controller to Louise last year – and I know Riley the Rat Man does a good job, because we had a problem at the garden centre a couple of years ago, and he sorted it out for us,' Sybbie said.

'Doesn't the dead rat show that the bait was working?' Georgina asked.

'No. I mean, there probably would have been some bait in the grain store, but that would have been just dotting the i's and crossing the t's. Riley would have checked all the entry points and blocked them up so the rats couldn't get into the grain store in the first place,' Sybbie explained. 'A rat even making it into the grain store doesn't sit well with me.'

'Jodie said she thought it was odd the whole class was ill at the same time, too,' Georgina said. 'Thinking back to when Will and Bea were little, I remember a couple of the kids would come down with a bug first, and then it'd go through the class in a kind of wave. I can't ever remember an entire class being sick all at the same time.'

'Neither can I, from when Giles was small,' Sybbie said. 'For the whole class to be ill at once, I'd suspect food poisoning. But it's very unlikely they all ate exactly the same thing.'

'Usually, I'd agree with you. But Harry said Louise gave them warm sausage rolls before the tour started,' Georgina mused. 'So they did all eat the same thing.'

'Could someone have interfered with the sausage rolls?' Sybbie asked. 'Because that would explain the kids all being sick. Louise obviously knows about food safety and has a hygiene certificate for the bakery. She's as hot on hygiene as Cesca is, or else Cesca would never have allowed her to supply the farm shop,' Sybbie added, sounding fiercely protective of Cesca and her decision to use Louise as a supplier. 'I think the only way something could have been wrong with the sausage rolls was if someone had interfered with them.'

'Nobody's doubting Cesca's attitude towards food safety,' Georgina hastened to reassure her friend. 'And that's a fair hypothesis. But you know how Colin questions everything. It's also strange that Louise and the two parent helpers weren't ill.'

'Maybe they didn't eat the sausage rolls,' Sybbie suggested.

'Maybe,' Georgina agreed. 'But if it was the sausage rolls that made everyone ill, why would anyone have meddled with them?'

'To make people ill. Perhaps someone's trying to frame Louise, and cause difficulties for her business?' Sybbie suggested.

'It's a theory, but I think you might be stretching it a bit, Sybbie,' Georgina said gently. The mysteries they'd solved together had been cold cases, and she knew Sybbie had enjoyed untangling the puzzles.

'Or maybe I'm not,' Sybbie said, her voice clipped to show she'd taken offence at Georgina's suggestion. 'When I told Cesca why you weren't coming to see us, yesterday, she mentioned that Louise has been having problems over the last few months. People have been spreading rumours. Silly stuff, about things being moved about in the bakery when nobody was there, and some old story about a mad miller murdering someone years ago.'

'*Murder?*' Georgina asked. 'Who, and when?'

'Cesca didn't know. She said it was all just gossip.' Sybbie sighed. 'Actually, Georgie, you're probably right and I'm stretching it a bit. Sorry for snapping at you. And that thing about the murder is probably some old tale that's got twisted over the years and was meant to explain how the mill ended up as a derelict heap in the first place.'

'Because it was abandoned after a murder, you mean? I think the truth is likely to be a lot more prosaic. Whoever ran the mill in the late eighteen hundreds couldn't do it profitably enough, once the rail network made transport easier and steam engines made mechanisation of milling easier,' Georgina said. 'After we talked about maybe putting together an article yesterday, I did a little bit of research into windmills in Norfolk. In the early eighteen hundreds, there were more than four hundred windmills across the county. Most of them have either been demolished or are derelict, and it seems there are only a handful still in working order.'

'It's almost tempting to believe that the gossip is the truth and there really *was* a murder at the mill. It might even be worth asking Doris if she knows anything about the mill's history, or if she could find out more about it for us,' Sybbie suggested.

Doris, the ghost of the eighteen-year-old girl who had died after falling down the stairs at Rookery Farm more than half a century ago, could talk to Georgina through her hearing aids, and had helped Georgina and Sybbie solve several cold cases over the previous couple of years. Although Georgina was the only one who could actually hear Doris's voice, Sybbie knew about Doris's existence and had talked with her, with Georgina acting as an intermediary.

'I'm not sure it works that way,' Georgina said. 'I think whoever died and wants the truth told about their death is the one who contacts Doris, not the other way round. Especially as we're not sure whether anyone did even die at Great Wenborough Mill. But all right – I'll ask her all the same.'

'Maybe we should check with Billy the butcher, too, to see if there's anything in the village history archives,' Sybbie said. 'I'm sure he'd be happy to help, especially as I know he supplies meat to the bakery. If someone is interfering with the sausage rolls, making people ill, that's going to have folk pointing a finger at him, too. And you know how quickly rumours and gossip spread.'

'I agree. And we need to talk to Louise,' Georgina said.

'You said yesterday about running a feature on the mill. That might be a nicer way of – well, *interfering*,' Sybbie said. 'Because that's what we're doing, isn't it?'

'Yes,' Georgina admitted. 'I'm pretty sure I can place the feature. Since you and Cesca know Louise already, it makes sense if one of you could talk to her and ask if she would like to show us round and let me take photographs.'

'I could put it to her that it'd be a case of two local businesses supporting another – her bakery and the mill, plus you with your photography,' Sybbie said, even though Georgina was semi-retired. 'Excellent. I'll call her now and let you know what she says.'

A few minutes later, Sybbie texted Georgina to let her know that Louise would be happy to show them round the mill and for Georgie to take photographs the following lunchtime. And that there was a special request from Louise's son for Bert to accompany them.

Georgina smiled. Clearly Louise had checked her out before agreeing to do any interviews or photographs, and had looked at her website, where Bert had a page all of his own. *Very happy to do that*, she texted back.

THREE

'Tulips? How lovely. Thank you,' Georgina said, accepting the large bunch of multi-coloured blooms and kissing Colin. 'The colours are gorgeous.'

He smiled. 'I can't get stocks at this time of year, and I know you love tulips. Even if these ones are hothouse flowers instead of the ones that look pretty in Sybbie's garden.'

'It's still a bit too early for spring flowers to come up in the garden,' she said with a smile. 'Though I love them all. The snowdrops, the daffodils, the tulips, and then the bluebells just as spring slides into summer.' They'd taken Bert to walk among a carpet of snowdrops the previous spring. 'I was thinking, it might be nice to take Bert to see the bluebells when they're out, at the beginning of May. Blickling Hall's Great Wood is amazing. The bluebells at Foxley Wood are spectacular, too, but unfortunately they have a no-dog policy.'

'We can't go without Bert,' Colin said. 'I think we should take him to Blickling.' He grinned. 'And that means a cup of coffee and a cheese scone in the café, afterwards.'

Georgina rolled her eyes. 'Trust you to spot an opportunity for a snack! I'll just put these in water, and then I'll put the kettle on.' She bustled about the farmhouse's kitchen while Colin hung his waxed jacket on the coat rack in the hallway and returned to sit on one of the mismatched oak chairs at the ancient oak table. Bert sat at his feet, resting his chin on Colin's knee, and Colin made a fuss of the spaniel.

'How was your day, Georgie?' he asked.

'Good, thanks. I'm going to Great Wenborough Mill tomorrow with Sybbie, for a nosey round the renovations and to take some photos for a feature,' Georgina said.

'Great Wenborough Mill? Hmm.' He looked thoughtful.

'It'll be interesting,' Georgina said. 'And whatever bug the class picked up seems to have di—' She stopped mid-sentence, realising how inappropriate the words she was about to say would be, and noticing Colin's expression. 'Ah. Do I take it that you're dealing with poor Miss Hurst's case?'

'What do you know about it?' he asked.

Georgina took that as a 'yes'. 'She was the temporary teacher for Harry's class, while Melanie James is on maternity leave. She only started at the school last week.' She winced. 'How awful for her family. Poor woman. Jodie told me this morning that Miss Hurst had died and there's going to be a PM. I did tell her that was par for the course for an unexpected death.'

'What bug did the class come down with, do you know?' Colin asked.

His tone was very casual, but Georgina had a feeling that his question was anything but. She finished making the tea, placed both mugs on the table and pulled out the chair next to his. 'That's the thing. It seemed like one of the common winter vomiting bugs, except it was a bit odd because the whole class went down with it at the same time. There were a couple of parent helpers, but they weren't affected. Sybbie said she'd suspect food poisoning, except that she knows Louise Wilkins is very hot on hygiene. Louise supplies the farm shop with flour and also some of the bread while Cesca's on maternity leave,' she added.

'With a virus, I'd expect a few kids in the class to get it first, then most of them to come down with it, then there'd be a few stragglers right at the end,' Colin said, tracing a bell-shaped distribution curve with his finger on the surface of the kitchen table to illustrate his point. 'Have any other children in the school caught this bug, do you know, or is it limited just to that class?'

'As far as I'm aware, it's just Harry's class. Jodie would be able to tell you more,' Georgina said.

'Sybbie's got a good point. The pattern of illness among the children fits the profile of food poisoning rather than a virus, with all of them being ill at the same time,' Colin said. 'How's Harry doing?'

'Better. Actually, they all are, according to Jodie – except for poor Miss Hurst, obviously. But the parents are all keeping the kids off school for another day, just in case.'

'Hmm,' Colin said. 'And a couple of parent helpers who weren't affected. I'll check whether they ate the sausage rolls. And I'll let Sammy, the pathologist, know. It might be significant.' His frown deepened. 'In my experience, vomiting viruses tend to last for more than just a day. I wouldn't expect any of the kids to be feeling much better today.'

'Neither would I. I was meant to pop in to see Sybbie and Cesca yesterday,' Georgina said. 'I cancelled the visit, just in case I'd caught the bug from Harry.'

'Good call. You wouldn't want the baby to pick up anything nasty,' Colin agreed.

'When Sybbie told her I wasn't coming and why, Cesca mentioned to her that Louise had been having a few problems lately,' Georgina added. 'People spreading rumours about... well, ridiculous stuff.' Given that Colin was starting to come round to the idea of Doris's existence, Georgina didn't want to open that particular can of worms.

But Colin, ever the detective, raised an eyebrow and looked at her.

She sighed. 'It sounds like poltergeist activity. And there's a story about a mad miller who murdered someone there, many years ago. Except that was probably just a rumour.'

'I assume you've talked to Doris about it,' Colin said, his tone neutral.

Georgina was relieved that his habitual scepticism about Doris hadn't returned, since the last case the ghost had helped her to solve. It didn't mean that he was delighted about accepting the existence of ghosts, though. 'Yes. Nobody has asked her for help. As far as I'm concerned, tomorrow is simply about having a tour of the windmill and taking a few photographs.'

'And hoping that Bert doesn't find some bones?' he asked wryly. It was a fair comment; Bert had discovered a few bodies since he'd come to live with Georgina, and Georgina had ended up helping to solve the cold cases of the bodies he'd uncovered.

'Exactly,' she said. She paused. 'There was one other thing. Harry said there was a dead rat in the grain store. Sybbie had recommended the pest controller to Louise Wilkins, and she thinks it's odd there was a rat.'

'Isn't it more likely that the dead rat proves the bait was effective?' Colin asked.

'That's what I said. But, according to Sybbie, when you have a rat problem, the first thing the pest controller does is find the entry points the rats are using so he can block them up,' Georgina explained.

'Maybe he missed one,' Colin said. 'Or was Sybbie suggesting that rat poison was the reason the whole class was ill?'

'Harry said they all had warm sausage rolls at the start of the trip,' Georgina said. 'But the mill and the bakery have a five-star hygiene rating. As I said earlier, Louise is hot on hygiene. She has to be, for her business.'

'Hmm.' Colin picked up his phone. 'I'm going to drop Sammy a note now, with all this,' he said. 'If she hasn't already come to a conclusion, this might be useful as a lead for further investigations.'

On Wednesday lunchtime, Georgina drove to Little Wenborough

Manor to pick up Sybbie, with Bert safely harnessed in the back of her car.

'Louise says Sam – her oldest son – is a lot better today, but like the other parents she's keeping him off school until forty-eight hours after the last time he vomited,' Sybbie said once she'd climbed in. 'But he's thrilled you agreed to bring Bert. She needs to collect her other son and daughter from the primary school at quarter past three, but a couple of hours should be plenty of time to show us round the mill and do the photographs.'

'Thanks for organising this, Sybbie,' Georgina said.

'No problem. She could fit us in so quickly because Wednesday is half-day closing – which feels a bit odd, in this day and age, but it's how it was when I was a small child. I assume Doris is with us?' Sybbie asked.

'She is,' Georgina said. 'Partly because she remembers the windmill being totally derelict and she's interested to see what Louise has done with it, and partly because she's hoping to see the baby when I drop you back home.'

'Excellent,' Sybbie said. 'And of course you can see the baby, Doris.' She paused. 'Did you hear any of the stories about the mad miller and the murders, when you were young?'

As usual – because she was the only one who could hear Doris – Georgina relayed the answers. 'Yes. Like everyone else, she assumed it was just a story. She hasn't been contacted by anyone on the other side about the mill.'

'It probably was just a rumour,' Sybbie said. 'Or maybe not even that. Bernard said there's a murder ballad called "The Bloody Miller" about a miller's apprentice murdering a girl he'd made pregnant. Apparently, back in the late 1600s, Samuel Pepys made a huge collection of the broadsides that were sold by publishers wanting to make a bit of money on execution day, claiming to be the killer's last confession or their dying words on the gallows. They were often turned into songs, hence murder ballads.'

'"The Bloody Miller",' Georgina mused. 'Was it about Great Wenborough Mill?'

'No. Bernard said the original murder happened in Shropshire, but there's another song with almost identical details called "The Berkshire Tragedy", set in Wytham near Oxford. Since then there have been a few different versions, set in different places – including an Appalachian murder ballad called "Knoxville Girl". So a lot of places that used to have a windmill also have a story about a mad murderous miller who'd once worked there, seduced a local girl and murdered her – except the murders didn't actually happen.'

Sybbie's husband, Bernard, could be very nerdy about the most surprising things, and Georgina was pretty sure he'd done his research. Her feeling was confirmed when Sybbie added, 'There's a Norfolk version recorded by Harry Cox in Catfield, called "Eke-field Town". Which obviously doesn't sound anything like "Wen-borough", but Bernard thinks it's the sort of story that sticks to anywhere that once had a dilapidated mill. And didn't you say there used to be hundreds of mills across Norfolk? You know how local lore gets: it's far more exciting to have a distant murder as the cause of a building being deserted, than for it to be simply because the business stopped being viable and the owner ran out of money.'

'That's true,' Georgina agreed.

She parked in the small car park outside the mill and unclipped Bert's harness from the car, putting him back on his lead. Sybbie held him while Georgina took out her camera bag. They knocked on the door of the pretty little cottage next to the mill, and a woman in her late thirties answered, her fair hair pulled back in a scrunchie at the nape of her neck.

'Lovely to see you, Sybbie,' she said, and smiled at Georgina. 'And you must be Mrs Drake, the photographer.'

'Do call me Georgie,' Georgina said, smiling back. 'And this is Bert.'

'This is Sam,' Louise said, introducing them to the young fair-haired boy with serious grey eyes and freckles who'd come to join her at the door. 'He's going to stay on the ground floor of the mill with Bert while I take you round and show you how it all works.'

The mill was an enormous tower built from red bricks. It was five storeys tall, with a white cap shaped like an upside-down boat, with four white sails on the front and a small circular fan on top of the cap. A vertical line of white-framed windows with nine rectangular panes marked each storey; on the ground floor, there was a stable door, painted white and with black iron hinges stretching across it, and immediately above it on the first floor was a second stable door.

'They've got the same kind of doors on the opposite side,' Louise said, 'so at any time you can go in and out of the mill – or bring sacks of grain in and out – without being hit by the sails.'

'The sails aren't fixed to the outside of the mill, then?' Sybbie asked.

'No – the windshaft connects to the driveshaft underneath the cap. The fantail at the top of the mill turns the cap so the sails always face the oncoming wind,' Louise explained. 'Let's go in, and I can show you how it all works.'

She unlocked the mill; the room in the base of the tower was surprisingly large, with a narrow ladder leading up to an entrance in the wooden floor of the next storey.

'Am I allowed to give Bert a treat?' Sam asked.

'I'm sure he'd love that,' Georgina said, pleased that the boy had asked first rather than assuming it was fine.

Sam took a dog biscuit from his pocket and made Bert proffer a paw for it.

'He does that with the neighbour's dog,' Louise said with a wistful smile. 'He'd love a dog of his own, but Hugo is away so much and Annie isn't keen on dogs.'

'Annie?' Sybbie asked.

'Our nanny,' Louise said, and sighed. 'Really, the children are too old now to need a nanny, but the waiting lists for childminders around here are so long. Annie's probably more of a housekeeper-cum-minder nowadays than a nanny, but I think she finds Norfolk a bit too quiet. My mother-in-law, Marion, has been staying with us for a few weeks so the builders can sort out the asbestos they found in her ceiling when they investigated a leak, but they're not really company for each other.'

'Annie's mean. And she's rude about Gran's cooking. Gran's a better cook than she is, too,' Sam muttered, but was quelled by a look from his mother.

'Annie looks after us all very well. And I'm grateful for the help. I shouldn't be talking about her behind her back.' Louise shook herself, and shepherded Sybbie and Georgina over to a large board which had a cut-through diagram of the mill and its machinery. 'We've got five floors here. The windshaft is under the cap, and it drives the upright shaft for the millstones. Going down from the top, there's a dust floor under the cap, the bin floor where we store the grain, the stone floor where we mill the grain, and the meal floor where we collect the milled grain. Plus this floor, which would have been the office, and it's where the sacks of grain begin their journey.' She indicated a chain which led through a trapdoor; meanwhile Georgina was snapping photographs as Louise pointed out the features of the mill. 'This is the hoist. You put a hook through the sack and attach the other end to the hoist, pull a string, and the hoist hauls the grain to the top of the mill.' She attached a sack of grain to the hoist. 'The old measures were used even after the second world war – four bushels to a coomb, which is a sack of grain, or just over two hundredweight. In modern terms, that's about two hundred and forty pounds, or a hundred and ten kilos. There were twenty coombs to the last, and this mill could grind four to five lasts a week.'

'Bushels, coombs and lasts. It sounds like another world,' Sybbie said.

'It really was,' Louise said. 'Every town had at least one mill, and all the neighbouring farmers brought their corn in sacks to the mill to be ground. Before steam engines and generators were available to power the mills, it meant the millers could only work the millstones when the wind was blowing – and that could end up being the middle of the night.'

'There wouldn't be much light coming through the windows at night, even if the sky was clear,' Georgina said.

Louise nodded. 'Even if they had a glass lantern to protect a candle flame, a candle doesn't give much light – and it's not the best idea to use a flame when there's highly combustible dust floating everywhere.'

'Margaret remembers her father having to put out a fire at night, in 1835,' Doris whispered into Georgina's ear. 'She would have been about eleven at the time. She helped him with the milling.'

Margaret, the miller's daughter – and Doris was the first one to mention her name. If her ghost *was* still here and talking to Doris, did this mean that there really had been a murder at the mill in the 1800s? Not that Georgina could ask just then, but she gave a brief nod to acknowledge what Doris had told her.

'It sounds dark and rather dangerous,' Sybbie said. 'Imagine trying to work in those conditions.'

'Let's just say I'm very grateful for electricity,' Louise said, with a wry chuckle. 'And I wouldn't have liked to rush up and down these ladders in a storm. They're a bit on the narrow side, as well as steep, and I think it would have been easy to lose your footing.'

'So you had to restore the whole building?' Georgina asked.

'Pretty much. I can show you the photographs I took of the building before I started. The sails had been taken off the mill and the cap was in ruins. It probably makes more sense if we climb to the top and work our way down,' Louise suggested. 'I brought a sack of wheat in earlier so I could show you what happens on each floor. I'll just run it up to the top.' She checked the sack was securely attached to the hoist, pulled the rope, and the trapdoor in the floor above opened so the sack could travel upwards through it. 'Amazing what you can do with a tiny bit of string,' she said with a smile.

The ladder leading to the next floor was quite narrow, and for a moment Georgina wondered if she'd be able to squeeze through the opening, but she made herself do it, following Louise and

Sybbie through narrower and narrower rooms until finally they were up on the bin floor at the top of the mill.

Louise talked them through the machinery in each room, showing Georgina and Sybbie how the chutes worked and the grain travelled down from floor to floor, being cleaned, milled and then finally dressed so it was split between wheaten flour, wholemeal flour and bran. In between, Georgina took more photographs of the machinery and of Louisa demonstrating.

Georgina peered out of the stable door. 'There's quite a drop. Is there some kind of hoist here so you can lower the sack of flour outside?'

'No. I don't have any pictures from here, but one of the other mills in the area was working right up to the second world war, and the owners told me it was common to use a wide plank as a kind of chute between the mill and the farmer's cart,' Louise said. 'The miller or the assistant would slide the sacks down the plank, and the farmer would be at the bottom, standing on the cart, to stack the sacks on the cart, and then push the plank back up into the mill.'

'I can't believe how noisy it is,' Sybbie said, 'and that it actually shakes the floor when the stones are turning.'

'Only the runner stone – the one at the top – turns,' Louise said. 'The bedstone, the one at the bottom, stays still.'

Sybbie and Louise walked on, and Georgina stayed where she was so she could have a quick conversation with Doris without Louise noticing. 'What can you tell me about Margaret?'

'Margaret Chorley, her name was,' Doris whispered into the silence as the millstone stopped turning. 'She was hanged for murder in 1845, when she was only twenty-one.'

Uh-oh. Did this mean there was a chance that Bert might find human remains in the windmill, the way he'd done at other sites under Doris's direction? Usually Doris was contacted by someone who'd been murdered and needed their story uncovered. If Margaret had been hanged for murder, why would she be the one asking for the story to be told, rather than the victim?

Before Georgina could ask, Doris added, 'Except she wasn't the killer.'

Which explained a lot. It sounded as if Margaret Chorley might have been framed, and needed help to find out who the real murderer was.

Sybbie knew about Doris and was used to Georgina passing on whatever Doris had just told her; but Louise didn't, so Georgina couldn't ask any more about Margaret without risking Louise hearing and then needing to have an awkward conversation. She frowned, hoping that Doris would take it as a sign that she'd heard and needed more information.

'Margaret's not buried here, by the way,' Doris added. 'She's at Norwich Castle – that was the city prison back in her day, and they buried people there after they'd been hanged at the castle.'

Well, that answered her next question. But if there were no bones to uncover at the mill, what did Margaret want them to find? Georgina wondered.

As if Doris guessed at the question, she added, 'I've been talking to Margaret. She moves things about in the mill – something needs to be found which proves her innocence.'

Which explained the rumours about poltergeist activity, but the 'something' that needed to be found was much too vague. Georgina couldn't ask anything now, without giving a lot of explanations that Louisa might not believe; but she could try another tack. 'Do you know much about the families who lived here over the years, Louise?' she asked when she'd caught up with Louise and Sybbie.

'It's on my to-do list to research them,' Louise said, 'but I've spent most of my time here so far on the physical restoration and getting the bakery business up and running, in between parenting.'

Sybbie looked at Georgina with a raised eyebrow, clearly asking if Doris had told her something. Georgina gave a small nod to let her know that she had.

'There are only twenty-four hours in a day,' Georgina said

lightly. 'Though when you're a parent you often wish there were more.'

'Tell me about it,' Louise said ruefully. She finished giving Georgina and Sybbie the tour of the mill, and they all climbed back down the final ladder to the ground floor.

'Do you want to see the grain store?' Louise asked.

'It might be good, for completion's sake,' Georgina said.

'There aren't any rats in it,' Sam piped up. 'Not like that one, the other day.'

Louise's mouth compressed. 'There shouldn't have been a rat then, either.'

'When we had our rat problem at the garden centre,' Sybbie said helpfully, 'Riley was very keen to check out all the entry points and make sure the rats couldn't get in.'

'Which is exactly what he did here,' Louise agreed. 'You and Cesca said he was very thorough, and you were right. I asked him to come over yesterday and have a look to see if he might have missed something when he did the original survey.'

'What did he think?' Georgina asked.

Louise waited until they were in the grain store and Sam was out of earshot. 'He thought the rat was brought in deliberately.' She bit her lip. 'I'm trying not to be paranoid, but I'm beginning to think someone wants me to fail. All those rumours starting up about some mad miller from years ago, the dead rat in the grain store, the children being ill, and now that poor teacher dying. The police have already been to see me and I've told them everything I know. But I made those sausage rolls myself. I'm meticulous about food safety, because I want to keep my customers happy and my business running. The hygiene team from the council is coming later this afternoon.'

'Do you think you've made an enemy of someone?' Sybbie asked.

'I have no idea,' Louise said, sounding frustrated and miserable at the same time – as if she'd asked herself that very question over and over and had failed to come up with an answer. 'I know sometimes it's hard to be accepted when you move into a rural community, especially if you're from London and everyone thinks you're taking houses and jobs from local people, but I honestly thought we were settled here. I thought people were pleased that we've brought the old mill back to life. The kids are all at school here – well, Isla's at the preschool, but that feeds into the primary school – and they seem to be getting on well with everyone. I have regular customers who make a point of coming in for a chat. Even Marion seems to have made friends, and she's only here temporarily – she's gone to Norwich today with a couple of ladies she met through the WI.' She looked anguished. 'It's horrible to think that I've made an enemy of someone and I don't have a clue who they are or what I've done to upset them.'

'Maybe you're not the problem,' Georgina said. 'As you say, sometimes rural communities find it difficult to come to terms with incomers. I moved here from London, too. I probably moved to Little Wenborough about the same time you arrived at Great Wenborough.' But nobody in the village had made her feel unwelcome or tried to damage either her photography business or the holiday let at Rookery Barn. She'd felt accepted in the village right from the start.

'I just want it all to stop, whatever it is,' Louise said. 'And I can't say a word in front of the children. I don't want to worry them.'

'What about your husband? Does he have any idea?' Sybbie asked.

Louise grimaced. 'Hugo still works full-time in London. He's shifted his hours a bit so he's here from Friday teatime to Monday breakfast, but... Well, I'm not sure village life is what he wants anymore.'

'But it's what you want?' Georgina asked gently.

'I love the mill. It felt like my place from the moment I first saw it,' Louise said. 'I love doing what I do. It's not the same in London, where I'm just one of a dozen bakeries on the high street trying to come up with an idea to make my business different from everyone else's.' She wrinkled her nose. 'Oh, ignore me. Let's go and have a hot drink, and I'll answer any more questions you might have.'

Back in the kitchen of Mill Cottage, Louise put the kettle on, and Sam continued to make a fuss of Bert.

'Sorry, it's a bit cramped in here at the moment,' Louise apologised.

The room was smaller than her own kitchen at Rookery Farm, Georgina thought, though it had the same red pamment-tiled flooring as hers, and the same monkey-tailed latches at the window. The cabinets were modern and cream-coloured, with a washing machine and tumble dryer visible underneath the maple worktops. At the far end of the kitchen, there was a huge American-style fridge plus an extendable table with six chairs crammed round it.

'We've had to move the dining table in here to give Marion a downstairs bedroom,' Louise explained.

'Dad moved my bed downstairs for her,' Sam added. 'I'm sleeping on a camp bed.'

'Because Gran's older than you and she'd find the camp bed uncomfortable and hard to get in and out of,' Louise said. 'And you're a good boy not to make a fuss about it.'

Sam blushed.

'Can I offer you a chicken-and-herb sausage roll?' Louise asked, taking a lidded storage box from the fridge.

At the word 'sausage', Bert sat nicely and looked hopeful.

Georgina and Sybbie exchanged a slightly nervous glance.

'It's a completely fresh batch,' Louise said. 'Everything I made yesterday went straight in the bin as soon as I heard the news.' Her expression was tense; clearly she'd seen the look they'd shared and realised why they were both slightly anxious about accepting the offer.

'I ate one this morning, when they came out of the oven,' Sam said.

And he looked right as rain, Georgina thought, whereas the children on Monday had all become ill very quickly. 'That'd be lovely. Thank you,' she said.

The relief on Louise's face – that she wasn't being judged and found wanting – made Georgina want to give her a hug.

'It's going to be all right,' she said gently.

'I'm not so sure. Everyone's talking,' Louise said, her eyes haunted. 'About how all the children were ill. About poor Miss Hurst. And only the parent helpers didn't get ill because they didn't eat the sausage rolls – they're both on a New Year's diet.'

Which answered another question, Georgina thought, filing it away to tell Colin later.

'You didn't do anything wrong, Mum,' Sam said loyally. 'Like Gran said, it's not your fault everyone got ill. It's not your fault Miss Hurst died, either.'

'No,' Louise said, clearly trying to be brave and positive for her son's sake, but Georgina could tell from the younger woman's expression that Louise *felt* as if it were her fault.

'Can Bert have a sausage roll, Mrs Drake?' Sam asked.

'A little bit of one,' Georgina said. 'Break a little corner off for him, and get him to ask you nicely for it.'

Sam looked thrilled when Bert sat and lifted a paw to say 'please'. And even Louise smiled.

'That's one lovely dog you have there,' she said, looking wistful.

Georgina scratched the top of Bert's head. 'Yes. I'm very lucky.'

FOUR

When Louise needed to leave to pick up her two younger children from school and nursery, Georgina drove Sybbie back to Little Wenborough Manor.

'Fill me in on what Doris told you at the mill,' Sybbie said as soon as they'd left.

'Margaret Chorley was the miller's daughter. She was hanged for murder at Norwich Castle in 1845, at the age of twenty-one, and was buried at the castle,' Georgina said. 'Doris doesn't know much more than that – well, except that Margaret didn't kill anyone. But apparently the rumours of things moving around the mill are true. It's Margaret, because she's trying to find something that will prove her innocence.'

'Normally it's the murder victim who contacts Doris, not the person accused of the murder,' Sybbie said. 'And normally there are bones for Bert to find and we can link them back to a paper trail. What are we looking for this time, Doris?'

'Doris doesn't know, either, at this point,' Georgina confirmed. 'I guess the first thing we need to do is see what we can find out about Margaret Chorley.'

'There might be something in Amelia's commonplace book or her diary in the Manor archives,' Sybbie said. Like many women of the time, Amelia Walters, Bernard's great-great-great grandmother, had kept a commonplace book; hers contained recipes, home remedies, handwritten copies of poems, notes of exhibitions and newspaper clippings, along with photographs and sketches. Sybbie and Georgina, together with Georgina's daughter, Bea, had pored through its pages the previous summer to help solve the mystery of a guest at the manor house disappearing without a trace.

'Plus we can ask Billy the Butcher if there's anything in the local history society's papers,' Georgina agreed.

She turned into the Manor's drive. As always, her breath caught at the first sight of the house. Built in the shape of an E, with stepped gable ends, stone mullioned windows and barley-sugar twist chimneys at either end of the red-tiled roof, it looked as if it belonged in a TV costume drama series. Even in winter, without the gorgeous purple wisteria flowers that graced its porch in the summer, the house was stunning. 'I love your house,' she said.

Sybbie grinned. 'I love the garden even more. Now, if we could only find that Red Book to prove that Repton designed it...'

'One day,' Georgina teased.

'Let's pop in and see Cesca and the baby, before we start digging through the archives,' Sybbie suggested, and Georgina parked outside the farmhouse rather than the manor house.

Francesca was delighted to see them, immediately switching the kettle on to make coffee, and Georgina was delighted to have a cuddle with Elizabeth, who promptly fell asleep in her arms at Francesca's kitchen table. The baby definitely looked like her mother, with the same beautiful dark eyes, and she was starting to get that delicious chubbiness babies developed. When she started smiling, Georgina thought, Elizabeth would have the kind of dimples that would make even the most sensible person want to babble baby-talk so the baby would smile and laugh.

'She's so gorgeous,' Doris said wistfully, at almost the same time that Francesca asked, 'Is Doris with you?'

'Yes,' Georgina said, smiling. 'She says Lizzie's gorgeous, too.'

'She certainly is,' Francesca said, beaming. 'How did you get on with Louise?'

'The mill's really interesting,' Georgina said. 'I took a ton of photographs as she showed us round. And Louise herself is really nice.'

'Dearest ma-in-law told me about that poor teacher dying,' Francesca said. She cut them all a slice of her famous lemon cake. 'That's so sad. Do you think someone could really be trying to make out that Louise gives customers – and kids – something that would make them ill, or even kill them?'

'I didn't get the impression she's the sort who'd want to make a whole bunch of children ill, including her own son, so it has to be someone trying to frame her. Can you think of anyone who'd want Louise out of Great Wenborough?' Sybbie asked.

'No,' Francesca said. 'I can't think of anyone. As a supplier, she's reliable. She's not really anyone's main competitor, either. There's enough business for all of us. Customers like her bread – and her sausage rolls and cheese scones.' She frowned. 'Obviously she must have got on the wrong side of *someone*. But who, and why, I have no idea.'

The rest of the conversation revolved around the baby, and Sybbie quickly washed up the mugs and plates before she and Georgina went back to the Manor House.

While Sybbie went to get Amelia's commonplace book from the manor's archives, Georgina watched Max and Jet, Sybbie's beloved black Labradors, chase around the garden with Bert. Still smiling at the dogs' antics, she rang Billy, Little Wenborough's butcher and head of the local history society. 'I'm trying to track down an alleged murder in Great Wenborough from 1845. Do you think there might be something about it in the local history society's papers, Billy?' she asked.

'Ooh, it rings a bit of a bell,' he said. 'There might be something in Mackie's *Annals*. Charles Mackie was a journalist who went through all the nineteenth-century issues of the *Norfolk Chronicle* and wrote out all the notable events. If you look up the entries for

1845, that'll help you narrow it down as to when the murder was reported in the papers, and then you'll be able to read what the journalists heard in court. The trial itself would have been held in Assizes Week. The main one was in the summer, usually the third or fourth week of July, but some years there was a spring assizes in April. You'd need to go to the library or the Records Office to see the newspapers, unless your Bea has some kind of log-in on one of the press sites.'

'Thanks,' Georgina said. 'I'll check with her.'

'Send me the details you've got,' Billy said, 'and I'll have a look for you in what we have here.'

'I don't actually have much more than a name and the year, right now,' Georgina admitted. 'Margaret Chorley, 1845. She was the miller's daughter, if that helps.'

'And she looks so sad,' Doris said. 'She can't remember much, but she swears she didn't murder anyone, even though she loathed Herbert Forrest.'

Who was Herbert Forrest? Georgina wondered. The person who was murdered at the mill?

'She's looking for something that will prove her innocence,' Doris continued. 'That's why she's moved things around in the windmill.'

Not that Georgina could explain that to Billy, or how she knew. She nodded to let Doris know that she'd heard.

'Ah.' Billy coughed. 'Would this have anything to do with the "mad murdering miller" gossip that's been going round the village?'

'Possibly,' Georgina said. 'Though you know what legends are like.'

'People change a bit or add a bit every time they tell the story,' Billy agreed. 'I reckon someone's got it in for Louise Wilkins,' he added darkly. 'There's no way she'd store sausage rolls so they'd go off and make someone ill. That,' he said, 'or someone's got it in for *me*, because everyone knows she buys the pork and chicken for her sausage rolls from me. Actually, Georgie, I won't wait until tonight

– I'll go and have a look for you now. Is this the best number to call you on?'

'Yes, please,' Georgina said.

'Right you are. And give your Bert a pat from me. I'll make sure my Sheena knows there's a sausage with his name on it next time you're in the shop.'

'Thank you. I will,' Georgina promised.

As Georgina finished the call, Sybbie came back to the kitchen with Amelia's diary and the commonplace book. 'Do you have a preference for which one you'd like to work through?' she asked.

'Either,' Georgina said. 'We know from Doris that Margaret was hanged in 1845, and Billy says the trial would have been held during Assizes Week, which he thinks is usually the second half of July – unless there was an April assizes as well, that year. She might have been held at the prison for a few months before the trial, so the murder must have happened sometime before July 1845 Assizes, and then she must have been hanged a few days after the trial.' She drummed her fingers on the kitchen countertop. 'I think we need to start from January 1845, so we don't miss anything.'

'I'll do the commonplace book, then,' Sybbie said. 'Let's go to the dining room. Is Doris still with us?'

'Yes,' Georgina confirmed.

'So if we come up with questions, Doris, you'll be able to talk to Margaret for us?'

Again, Georgina repeated Doris's answer. 'Yes.'

Sybbie's dining room was very grand, painted a deep red with rich brocade curtains. There was an ornate stone fireplace with some of Sybbie's collection of Staffordshire china dogs flanking the ormolu clock on the mantelpiece, and there were various gilt-framed landscapes and portraits on the walls.

The polished oak dining table sat sixteen, so there was plenty of room to spread out the papers. Sybbie and Georgina sat side by side in companionable silence, working their way through the ancient pages. Sybbie had brought pencils and a couple of notepads from the archive room, so they could make notes without risking any damage to the diary or the commonplace book.

'Here's something in Amelia's diary,' Georgina said. 'April 1845. "Terrible news from the village. Herbert Forrest's young son died, thought to have been poisoned by a cake."' And Forrest was the name that Doris had mentioned earlier, she remembered.

'Oh, no,' Sybbie said. 'I can't imagine anyone deliberately poisoning a child. It must have been an accident. I know this sounds a bit improbable, but the only thing I can think of is maybe the cake was intended as bait for rats and they didn't realise the child had eaten some?'

'Amelia doesn't go into any details, but I can't imagine anyone going to the trouble of baking a cake for a rat,' Georgina said.

'Maybe it was stale and someone sprinkled the poison onto it, or mixed it into the jam if it was a Victoria sponge. Rats like sugar, don't they?' Sybbie suggested.

'Thankfully, I've never had to deal with rodents, so I wouldn't know,' Georgina said. 'But this case feels odd. We know Doris is usually contacted by the victim rather than the murderer. Yet Margaret was the one accused of the murder, found guilty in court and hanged for it.'

'She didn't do it,' Doris reminded them.

'But why were the judge and jury convinced she did it?' Georgina asked. 'Did she make the cake?'

'If she didn't, then who put the poison in the cake, and how?' Sybbie asked. 'But we have lots of questions now. I also want to know who this Herbert Forrest was. What connection did Margaret have with him, or the child? Why would anyone want to poison him or his family? And if Amelia meant Little Wenborough by "the village", what was the connection with the mill at Great Wenborough, and why did they think Margaret was the one who killed the little boy?'

'Who baked the cake? Did they know any of the ingredients contained poison? Did the little boy maybe take a piece of cake after he'd been told not to touch it?' Georgina asked, jotting all the questions onto a list. 'Doris, can you take these questions back to Margaret and see if they jog her memory at all?'

'Of course I will,' Doris said. 'But I'll hang about here for a little longer, in case you find something else in the diary or the commonplace book.'

'Good idea,' Georgina said.

Just as she'd finished noting down the questions, Billy rang her. 'I've got something for you,' he said. 'You probably already know that broadsides are the accounts of the crime that printers sold after the executions. Well, we've got one in our archives, telling Margaret Chorley's story. I *knew* it rang a bell.'

'Hang on a sec, Billy – I'm with Sybbie right now. I'm going to put my phone on speaker so we can both hear you,' Georgina said.

'Afternoon, Lady Sybbie,' Billy said when Georgina had switched the phone from her hearing aids to the speaker.

'Afternoon, Billy,' Sybbie responded. 'What have you got for us?'

'The broadside – the printed account of the crime. Printers used to sell them for a ha'penny, right after the execution. They're only printed on one side of the page because the paper's very thin, to keep costs as cheap as possible. They're even more sensational than the gutter press is nowadays, and there's always a moral warning to the reader at the end,' Billy explained. 'They normally have a verse or two and sometimes a woodcut of the execution itself, or some dramatic scene about what happened. There's a woodcut at the top of this one, showing Margaret's body hanging, framed in the gallows between the two gatehouse towers at Norwich Castle.'

'They hanged criminals outside the castle rather than inside?' Georgina asked.

'That's right. So people could see justice being done. They used to build the gallows on the bridge, just behind the gates of the towers. People would stand on what used to be the old castle ditches, and watch the condemned person being hanged. The ditches were flattened in the eighteenth century, and the area was made into the cattle market,' Billy said. 'It's where they'd hold the fair – and, as I said, where people would watch the hangings.'

'That's really gruesome,' Sybbie said.

'Worse than that,' Billy said. 'Back when Margaret was hanged, the hangman still used an ordinary slipknot instead of a proper noose, so her neck wouldn't have broken instantly from the drop. She would have been strangled, and it might have taken her as long as twenty minutes to die. That's why they talk about people dancing on the end of a rope. Hanging day was often marked by a fair, so there would have been big crowds to watch. Hundreds, maybe even thousands of people. And afterwards the printers would sell the broadsides telling people all about the crimes, and the hangman would sell bits of the rope as good luck charms for gamblers. They sometimes even cut up the deceased's clothes and sold bits of that.'

'That's horrible,' Georgina said. 'Mind you, those were the days when people toured Bedlam because insanity was treated as entertainment, so I'm not entirely surprised.'

'I've photographed the broadside for you,' Billy said. 'Shall I email it to you?'

'Yes, please,' Georgina said.

'I'll send it to both of you. Text me your email addresses,' Billy said. 'And let me know what else you find out.'

'Of course we will,' Georgina said.

A few moments later, Georgina's phone pinged with an email from Billy, followed a second or two later by Sybbie's phone.

Sybbie opened the email, peered at the photograph and sighed. 'That print size is way too small for my eyes, even with my glasses. Let me get it up on my laptop so we have a bigger screen to work with.'

It didn't take her long to fire up the laptop, flick into her email program and bring up the photograph of the broadside.

Georgina shivered. 'That woodcut at the top is truly horrible. I don't know what's nastier – the sight of a body hanging on a gallows, or the crowd watching the spectacle, all gussied up in their

Sunday best. And look at that headline! "Mad miller, child killer" – that's the kind of thing you'd see in the tabloids today, stirring up hatred and resentment.'

'I thought Margaret was the miller's daughter, not the actual miller?' Sybbie asked. 'Though, according to this, she took over the mill from her father.' She scanned the words quickly. 'And the rest of the story is horrible. It says Margaret was in love with Herbert Forrest and they had an affair, but then he cast her off. Herbert's wife, Catherine, was an invalid who could only drink milk thickened with flour. Margaret thought that if she got rid of Catherine, she could take her place as Forrest's wife. She sent a parcel of flour sprinkled with arsenic to the house, thinking the cook would make it up for Catherine, who would then drink it and die.'

'But the cook didn't use the flour to make the milk drink for Catherine. Instead, she made a cake with it,' Georgina said, reading further. 'Herbert and Catherine's six-year-old son Daniel ate a piece and died.'

'It seems that nobody else ate any cake, or at least nobody else was killed by it,' Sybbie said. 'Maybe because Daniel was so young, he became ill very quickly after eating the cake and then everyone realised there was a problem. Why else would an entire household leave a cake untouched after it had been cut?'

'Catherine couldn't eat solid food, by the sound of it, so she wouldn't have eaten any. Maybe Herbert wasn't yet home from whatever he did for business,' Georgina said.

'What about the servants? Why didn't they eat any of the cake?' Sybbie asked, frowning.

'If it had been made for the family, maybe they felt they had to wait until they were told they could have the leftovers,' Georgina suggested.

'Were they scared of the cook, or of the master of the house?' Sybbie wondered aloud.

'Either or both. Maybe Herbert Forrest was one of these men who wanted everyone under his thumb – well, we've seen that a few times already in the cases of people we've helped,' Doris said.

'We have,' Georgina agreed. 'Billy said these broadsides tend to be sensationalist, though. What if Margaret wasn't in love with Herbert at all, and he was a neighbour who took a fancy to her and decided to take what he wanted? If Margaret, rather than her father, was working as the miller, it sounds as if her father wouldn't have been in a position to protect her.'

'We also don't know that she had anything to do with the poison in the first place – at least, not until we see the trial records or the newspaper reports, or hear what Doris can tell us,' Sybbie said. 'It says in the broadside that the flour was poisoned – but scientific analysis was much cruder then than it is now. How could they be so certain that the flour was the poisoned ingredient in the cake? It might have been in the sugar or the butter.'

'I think I've got more than enough to discuss with Margaret, for now,' Doris said. 'I'll be back when I can.'

A few minutes later, Bernard came into the dining room. 'That looks like Amelia's diary and the commonplace book,' he said. Clearly he remembered the investigation he'd helped with, because he added, 'Are you two working on a case?'

'The beginnings of one, I think,' Georgina said. 'Doris says Margaret Chorley was hanged for a murder she didn't commit, back in 1845. She was the daughter of the miller in Great Wenborough, aged twenty-one, accused of murdering a little boy with a poisoned cake. We've found a reference to the case in Amelia's diary, and Billy the butcher sent over the broadside sold after the execution.'

'A murdering miller. I'm guessing Sybbie's told you about the murder ballads already. In most of them, the miller – or his apprentice – murders a young woman he's made pregnant,' Bernard said. 'It's very unusual to have a miller's *daughter* being the murderer. If anything, I'd expect her to be the victim.'

'Sybbie told me about your murder ballads, yes,' Georgina said.

'Well, they're not really mine,' he said with a smile. 'What do you know about the case?'

'At the moment, we have a lot more questions than answers,'

Georgina said. 'The broadside suggests that Margaret intended to kill Herbert Forrest's wife, because she wanted to marry him, but instead Herbert's six-year-old son ate the poisoned cake.'

'The ballads are usually about a girl who was seduced and then cast off once she'd fallen pregnant,' Bernard said. 'Obviously this is very different. Where are you planning to look next?'

'We're going to look through the rest of 1845 in Amelia's diary to see if we can find any more relevant information,' Sybbie said.

'Then either look at the trial records, if we can get hold of them, or the newspaper reports,' Georgina said. 'Plus we can factor in whatever Doris can find out from Margaret.' Bernard, she'd discovered a few months before, was broad-minded enough to accept Doris's existence.

'Poison,' Bernard said thoughtfully. 'But you told me about all the children being ill, Sybbie, and that poor teacher dying. If they all ate the sausage rolls, that suggests the food was poisoned.'

'Louise also told us that the two parent helpers – who weren't ill – didn't eat a sausage roll because they were on a diet,' Sybbie added.

'Which supports the theory of poison,' Bernard said.

'Right now, we don't have the evidence to say what exactly made them ill. But if it *was* poison, who on earth would deliberately do that to a class of children?' Georgina asked.

'Colin's the one who needs to find that answer – that is, as you say, if it really was poison,' Bernard said. 'But it's easy to see a link between a case of poisoning in the 1800s and what happened this week. Are you going to fill him in on this?'

'I think,' Georgina said, 'I rather need to.'

FIVE

Georgina had just driven home and let Bert loose in the back garden when Doris said, 'We need to talk.'

'I'm listening,' Georgina said, unlocking the kitchen door. 'I take it you've spoken with Margaret?'

'All that stuff in that broadside wasn't true. The printer paid a local poet to write the verses, and they cobbled most of it together from a pile of other broadsheets the poet had written.'

'All the "let this be a warning to you not to do this, or you'll end up on the gallows too" stuff?' Georgina asked, taking off her coat and hanging it on the rack in the hallway.

'Yes. But, more to the point, Margaret wasn't in love with Herbert Forrest. Quite the opposite. She said he was a horrible, sweaty little man who looked like a toad, with bags under his eyes and a slimy mouth like a two-day-old fish,' Doris said.

'Definitely not the description of someone anyone would find attractive,' Georgina agreed, unable to repress a smile.

'No. He was a miller – at least, he started out as one, but...' Doris sighed. 'You studied *The Canterbury Tales* at uni, didn't you?'

'Yes, though Shakespeare was always more my thing,' Georgina agreed.

'So you know how Chaucer described the millers – both the one among the pilgrims who tells the smutty tale about Alison cheating on her husband with Nicholas the scholar, and the one in *The Reeve's Tale.*'

'Robin the miller – the pilgrim who tells the smutty tale having a go at carpenters – is stout and strong. Which, given that his job meant he was hauling around heavy sacks of grain and flour all day, isn't surprising,' Georgina said. 'If I remember rightly, he's also a bit ugly, liked his drink, and had a nose with a hairy wart. And Chaucer described him as having a golden thumb, implying that he was a cheat.'

'A lot of millers were accused of cheating their customers, using their thumbs to press on the scales and make a sack of flour look as if it weighed more than it actually did,' Doris said. 'According to Margaret, Herbert Forrest was one of the bad guys. He'd been accused of cheating on more than one occasion, but he always managed to wriggle out of it. Usually by paying off the magistrates,' she added, sounding disapproving.

Georgina sighed. 'Poor Margaret. I have a nasty feeling about where this might be going.'

'Her dad was ill,' Doris said. 'That's why she had to take over doing the bulk of the milling work. She'd helped him at the mill for years, doing the accounts and writing receipts and what have you, plus she'd learned how to work all the machinery, but she said he was starting to wander in his mind.'

'Does she mean he had the beginnings of dementia?' Georgina asked.

'It sounds like it, from what she told me,' Doris said. 'Anyway, Forrest had a bit of a roving eye. He cornered Margaret one night outside the Red Lion, when she'd got a neighbour to sit with her dad and she'd gone to the pub to fetch him some beer. Someone came out of the pub and she managed to get away from Forrest before he could do anything to her, but she was always aware of him watching her, and it gave her the creeps.'

'Was he involved with the poisonings?' Georgina asked.

'I don't know. That's all Margaret can remember at the moment,' Doris said. 'Though she's adamant that she wasn't the one who poisoned the little boy. She didn't like Forrest, but she would never, ever have hurt his child. She wasn't jealous of Catherine, either, whatever the newspapers claimed. Margaret didn't want anything to do with Forrest. She just wanted to help her dad and keep him as well as she could, and to keep the business going so she could afford to look after him.'

'I think I need to go to the archives and do some research,' Georgina said.

Bert suddenly gave a small wuff of pleasure and bounded to the kitchen door, wagging his tail.

'That's Colin getting out of his car,' Doris said. 'I'd better be off. We'll talk tomorrow and discuss anything else you've found that might help me to jog Margaret's memory.'

'All right. And thank you for all your help,' Georgina said.

A few moments later, Colin walked into the kitchen and greeted Georgina with a kiss. 'How did you get on at the mill today?' he asked.

'It was really interesting,' Georgina said. 'Louise took us through all the stages of milling. Then we started talking about the people who worked at the mill back in the 1800s.'

'You didn't call me,' Colin said, 'so I'm assuming that this time Bert didn't find any stray bones.'

'No. He spent his time at the mill playing with Sam – Louise's oldest – while Sybbie and I were doing the tour, and then Sam enjoyed feeding Bert a s-a-u-s-a-g-e r-o-l-l in Louise's kitchen.'

Despite the fact she hadn't said the words properly, Bert immediately sat, looking alert, and held up a hopeful paw.

Colin laughed. 'I have a feeling he's learned the spelling of the s-word.'

'It certainly looks like it,' Georgina agreed ruefully. 'Bert, you can't have another one today. Though I might pop in and buy some from the bakery tomorrow. Just to show Louise a bit of support.'

She looked at Colin. 'I'll put the kettle on, but dare I ask how the case is going?'

'The council's hygiene team was due to call on Louise today,' Colin said. 'I'm still waiting for some pathology results from Sammy, to see if Miss Hurst had some kind of underlying health condition that maybe even she didn't know about. That's the most likely explanation for her death.' He frowned as he took two mugs off the dresser and the milk from the fridge, then took them all over to the kettle. 'Even though I think the circumstances are a bit strange and it's highly unlikely that a whole class went down with a virus all at the same time – let alone their teacher dying from said virus – right now I don't have any evidence to prove that there's been any kind of wrongful act, or who might have done it.'

'In other words, you're stuck,' she said, filling the kettle at the sink. 'Well, I have a bit more information. The two parent helpers who weren't ill – apparently they said no to a sausage roll because they were sticking to a diet.'

'That,' Colin said, 'could be significant.' He made a note.

'I also learned something else today,' Georgina said. 'You know I thought all the stuff about the murdering miller at Great Wenborough was a mix-up with the old ballads? It turns out there really *was* a Victorian murder connected to the mill. Margaret Chorley, the miller's daughter, was hanged for murder in 1845.'

'Hang on.' Colin frowned as he sat down at the ancient oak table. 'I thought you said Bert didn't find any bones at the mill?'

'He didn't,' Georgina said. 'I have...' She paused, not quite sure how to put it. 'Other evidence,' she said carefully.

'Hmm,' Colin said.

She really didn't want a fight over this. To her relief, he took a different tack. 'Back in those days, most murderers were male. A female murderer was quite unusual. Would I be right if I said the murder weapon was poison?'

'Allegedly, yes,' Georgina said. 'Though I'm not convinced Margaret was the one behind the poisoning.'

'Because Doris told you?' Colin asked.

Here came the quarrel, she thought with an inward sigh. This had been a bone of contention between them for months, although Colin had seemed to be coming round to the idea of Doris's existence – mainly because he couldn't find any other reasonable explanation for why Georgina knew some things before she'd found the documentary evidence. When Georgina found herself in the process of crossing her arms defensively, she deliberately stopped herself, looking him straight in the eye instead. 'As you've asked me outright, I'll give you an honest answer. Yes. Doris told me.'

'All right,' Colin said.

No arguments? No quibbling over a point?

That meant he really was starting to accept that she was telling the truth.

'If she says Margaret didn't do it, and you're determined to uncover what really happened,' Colin continued, 'then you'll need to look at why Margaret was hanged and what the evidence was.'

It was solid advice, Georgina knew. 'At the moment, I'm still at the very early stages of finding out what happened,' she admitted. 'Most of the evidence I have is from Amelia Walters' diary and the photograph of a broadside that Billy the butcher sent over to me.'

'Broadsides being the historical equivalent of a scandal sheet, and you definitely can't rely on the details, because half of them would be made up to make the story even more sensational,' Colin said, rolling his eyes. 'The council's hygiene team is going to call on Billy as well, by the way.'

'No doubt because he supplied the pork and chicken for Louise's sausage rolls,' Georgina said with a sigh. 'Could someone have it in for Billy, as well as for Louise? Or is Billy the true target, and Louise is the collateral damage?'

'Either or both,' Colin said. 'At the moment, we haven't identified anyone who might have a grudge against Louise or Billy. Let's go back to this broadside Billy gave you. What did it claim?'

'That Margaret was in love with Herbert Forrest – except

Doris says she wasn't.' Georgina measured ground coffee into the cafetière and poured boiling water on top.

'Who was Herbert Forrest?' Colin asked.

'At the moment, I think he was a miller, but I need to look him up in the trade directories to see what exactly his business interests were,' Georgina said. 'I might have a session in the records office tomorrow. I'm making a list of questions.' She looked at him. 'Why did you say you thought it was poison?'

'Poison was seen mainly as a woman's weapon in Victorian times, probably because it didn't need the physical strength of other methods,' Colin said. 'The victim was usually the husband she wanted to get rid of, the lover who'd spurned her, or her rival.' He grimaced. 'Which is a horribly simplistic way of putting it, although a lot of the media wrote the stories that way because it suited their audiences. Real life is a bit more nuanced than that.'

'Husbands, lovers and rivals? None of those descriptions fits this case. Margaret wasn't married, and Forrest wasn't her lover. She didn't have a rival for his affections, either,' Georgina said. 'He was married, and the broadside claims his wife was the intended victim of the poisoning – but it didn't go as planned, and Herbert Forrest's six-year-old son died instead.' She explained what she'd learned about Catherine Forrest's ill health from the broadside, and how the poisoned flour had been made into a cake instead of adding it into Catherine's a drink.

'The local papers should give you a lot more information about the trial,' Colin said. 'Obviously the reporting will have some bias, especially in the descriptions of the accused and the witnesses, but the news coverage of the time tended to be more detailed than the actual trial reports were. You should get the witness statements more or less word for word, and hopefully some of the lawyers' arguments as well.'

'What about the trial records themselves?' Georgina asked.

'Most of the Assize records are kept at Kew. But I gather the way they're collected and listed really varies, depending on the district,' Colin said. 'I reckon the newspapers will be more helpful to you at this stage, and they're a lot easier to get hold of.'

'I think you're right,' Georgina said, stirring the coffee and pushing the plunger down before pouring the coffee into the mugs and adding milk to her own.

'You said Billy sent you a photo of the broadside. Can I take a look?' Colin asked as she brought the mugs over to the table, clearly interested in her cold case.

'Of course. I'll bring it up on my laptop, so you can read it on a decent-size screen.' She moved her laptop to the place next to Colin's chair and sat beside him.

'I've seen some of these before. I notice they went straight in with the woodcut at the top, with this one,' he said when she opened the file. 'Obviously it's not an actual sketch of Margaret – it's a standard pose, which the printer might tweak slightly and reuse. They would have printed the broadside on the day of the hanging and hawked it round the onlookers as a souvenir of the day.' He grimaced. 'Gruesome, but that's how life was back then.'

'Saturday, 9 August 1845,' she said, pointing out the date.

'And at the bottom we have the name of the printer – Robert Walker of St Miles, Coslany,' he said.

'I'm going to look him up in the trade directories, too,' Georgina said. 'Though I do know that St Miles' church is still on Coslany Street, so he would have been based somewhere nearby. Coslany was one of the original Saxon settlements that made up Norwich – known as Norwich Over-the-Water.'

'You and your local history. Have you been fossicking in Bernard's shelves again?' Colin teased gently.

She laughed. 'Busted. Though I have bought my own copies of the ones that really caught my attention.'

'Between Sybbie and her china dogs, and you with ancient books, I think they should be rolling out the red carpet in the antique shops and second-hand bookshops every time the two of you go to Holt.' Though the glint in Colin's eyes told Georgina that he was charmed rather than being disdainful. He seemed to enjoy her geeking out over local history almost as much as he enjoyed her quoting Shakespeare at him.

He smiled. 'If you find an address, let me know and I'll go and take a look next time I manage to get a lunch break in the office. If the building's still there, I can take some photographs for you, if you like.'

'Thank you,' she said.

'Given that we're both stuck,' he said, 'at least until tomorrow, can I take you to dinner at the Feathers?'

'That would be lovely,' Georgina said.

There was a soft wuff from under the table.

'Of course I'm not leaving you out, Bert,' Colin said, reaching under the table to make a fuss of the spaniel. 'And I'm sure there's going to be a sausage with your name on it in Hannah's kitchen.'

On Thursday, Georgina spent the morning at the Records Office on the outskirts of Norwich. She started with *White's History, Gazetteer, and Directory of Norfolk* from 1845. She knew from talking to Bea that each village would have a listing giving brief notes about the church and any notable buildings, and a note of the principal landowners. Larger towns would have notes about the mail delivery, public officers, courts, schools and railway stations. Private residents were listed in alphabetical order but tended to be mainly landowners, the gentry and the vicar. Business owners were listed in alphabetical order under the 'commercial' sections, including farmers, shopkeepers, publicans, doctors and bank managers.

Under the listings for Little Wenborough, as she'd expected, Georgina saw an entry for the vicar at St Edmund's church, and for William Walters, Lord Wyatt, of Little Wenborough Manor. There were also listings for several farmers, including at Rookery Farm, plus a wheelwright and a shoemaker. There were two pubs in the village – the Red Lion, which was still there, as well as the King's Arms, which had long since been turned into a private house – plus several shops: the butcher's, the grocer's, the black-smith's and the post office. The blacksmith had long gone, and the post office had amalgamated with the grocer's, but the butcher's was still proudly going strong.

Herbert Forrest was listed under the commercial section of Little Wenborough as a mill-owner and corn factor in Mill Street; though in the present day there were no traces of the former mill in Little Wenborough other than in the street name. Forrest was a mill-owner rather than a miller, she noted. So did that mean he hadn't worked the mill himself? Did he own more than one mill? That was a possible question for Margaret, if she couldn't find out in the archives.

A corn factor, she knew, was a dealer in grain. Thomas Hardy, rather than her beloved Shakespeare, came to mind: Donald Farfrae, Henchard's protégé and complete opposite in *The Mayor of Casterbridge*. Which of them had Forrest been more like? she wondered. Difficult, rigid and flawed like Henchard, or open and socially adept like Farfrae? Not that it made any difference now. Margaret Chorley had been hanged unfairly nearly two hundred years ago. It would be good to find out the truth.

Great Wenborough's listings included the vicar of St Mary's church and Edward Rutherford of Great Wenborough Hall – a surname she recognised from the historical case she and Sybbie had solved the previous summer, that had involved Bernard's family. Plus there were the usual farmers, pubs and shopkeepers. In the commercial section she saw 'Alfred Chorley and daughter, millers and bakers, The Croft'. Georgina had a feeling that by the time the directory had been printed, Margaret was doing most of the work and her dad was the miller in name only.

If her hunch was correct and Herbert Forrest owned other mills, which villages were they in? She turned to the trade direc-tory at the back, noting that millers were marked with a little symbol to show whether they were powered by water, wind or steam. There were only a handful of steam mills, and none of them were Forrest's. Under *Forrest, Herbert*, there was a list of villages whose names she recognised as being close to Great Wenborough. She'd already paid for a photography permit, and had one of her smaller digital cameras with her. She took a photograph of the relevant pages and wrote the details in pencil in her notebook.

Given the number of mills Forrest owned, had he heard rumours that Alfred Chorley was struggling, and thought that it would be easy to intimidate his daughter – who, as a young woman, would be vulnerable – into selling the mill to him at a ridiculously low price, so he could increase his empire on the cheap? At the moment, it was all speculation, but Georgina had a nasty feeling about this. And she really didn't like bullying and sharp practice.

She replaced the directory, and went to find Mackie's *Annals*. Amelia's diary had mentioned the death of Daniel Forrest in April 1845; sure enough, the *Annals* had a reference to an 'inquest into the death of Daniel Forrest, who was believed to have been poisoned'. She made a note of the date, and followed through to July to see what had happened in Assizes Week. The first mention was about an actress who 'appeared at Norwich Theatre in the Assize week performances'. Then there was a one-liner about the trial of Margaret Chorley for the murder of Daniel Forrest by poison on 23 July; she was found guilty. And under August it was noted that Margaret was hanged on Saturday 9 before a crowd of five thousand people.

She noted the dates and logged in to the family history website which had made some digitised newspapers available. 1845 wasn't one of the years digitised for one of the two newspapers she wanted, so she had to use one of the old microfilm readers in the archives instead. Even though she had the relevant dates, and the newspapers were only published once a week and had four pages each, the print on the pages was so tiny that it took her ages to find the article she needed. She enlarged them on the screen and took photographs rather than trying to transcribe them.

It wasn't fair to Bert to leave him at home alone for the entire day, so she decided to call it a day at that point and work on the articles at home.

Back in Little Wenborough, she took Bert for a walk so he could let off some steam. 'You know, Bert, it's about time we popped over to see Valerie.' Valerie Waring, one of Jodie's neighbours, was Bert's former owner, but had become frail and had needed to move to sheltered accommodation. Unable to keep Bert with her, she'd asked Jodie to help her find Bert a new home; Jodie had teamed up with Sybbie and Francesca to persuade Georgina to take him on.

'We'll take her some flowers,' she said. 'And a treat.'

Bert wagged his tail.

'I'll ring first, to check if she's free for a visit,' Georgina said.

Valerie was thrilled to hear from her, and even more delighted at the thought of a visit from Bert.

Georgina settled Bert into the back of the car and clipped his harness into the seatbelt. She picked up some daffodils from the farm shop, then called by the bakery in Great Wenborough.

Louise was behind the counter in the shop, which was empty, though the shelves were full of bread and the glass-covered display of sausage rolls and scones looked barely touched. The café in the next room wasn't busy, either; there was a single couple at one table drinking tea. Georgina suppressed a sigh. Clearly the village grapevine was focusing on the children's sickness rather than the fact that Louise had been visited by the council's hygiene team and they'd cleared her to continue business.

'I was going to ask how things were going,' Georgina said, 'but I can see for myself.'

'It's not great,' Louise said. 'Marion's been helping me out in the café, but I haven't needed her today. I've had two schools cancel planned visits over the next fortnight, too.'

'I'm sorry,' Georgina said. 'My contact at the paper says they'll run the piece the week after next in the lifestyle pages of the weekend magazine. They might run another version in the glossy monthly magazine, too. Hopefully that will help.'

'Thank you,' Louise said, but there was no sparkle in her smile.

Georgina really felt for the younger woman, whose dreams were clearly crumbling round her.

'Can I buy some sausage rolls, please?' she asked. 'I'm visiting an old friend – Bert's former owner. She loves spicy food, so could I have a couple of the chicken-and-chili sausage rolls for her, and half a dozen of the chicken-and-herb ones?' Colin could take them into the station as a Friday treat for his team, perhaps.

'Are you sure?' Louise asked.

'Definitely,' Georgina said. 'And I'll have a loaf of your rye bread, too.'

This time, she was relieved to see that Louise's smile was a bit more genuine.

Valerie was delighted by the visit and made a huge fuss of Bert. Georgina made tea and put the daffodils in a vase of water.

'Will you have one of the sausage rolls?' Valerie asked.

'Thanks, but no. I bought them for *you*,' Georgina said. 'Bert and I have both eaten too many already this week.'

'He never could resist sausages,' Valerie said. 'It was the only thing I ever knew him steal off a plate. I'd just turned round to get the mashed potato from the top of the stove one night, and when I turned back the sausages weren't there anymore. He'd scoffed the lot in a single gulp!'

'Greedy boy,' Georgina said affectionately, scratching the top of the spaniel's head. Bert looked completely unrepentant.

At the end of the visit, Georgina kissed Valerie's cheek and clipped Bert's harness into the back of the car, then headed home to do some more work on the article about the mill. But when she parked outside the farmhouse and opened the door to let Bert out, she realised she'd left the sausage rolls within his reach; all that was left was an empty bag and crumbs.

'Oh, *Bert*,' she said.

The spaniel's ears drooped, and he looked sorrowful.

'You fraud. I know you're not in the least bit sorry,' she said. 'All six of them! I don't think you're going to have room for any dinner tonight.'

Bert skulked into the kitchen when she'd opened the door, and lay down on his bed, his nose on his paws.

'It's pointless yelling at you, because it's not going to bring the sausage rolls back. I'm not angry with you,' she said, bending down and making a fuss of him. 'I'm cross with myself, though, for not putting them in the front of the car, out of your reach. And they're so rich that I really hope you're not sick from scoffing so much.'

Bert gave a lacklustre wag of his tail.

'Right – I'm going to do some work before I pick up the girls for Pilates tonight.' She refreshed his water bowl, then sat at the kitchen table and switched on her laptop. Bert didn't come to lie on her feet, the way he usually did, but she assumed that was because he was too full to move.

An hour later, her phone pinged with a message from the Pilates teacher. The class was cancelled that evening because she'd gone down with a bug.

'It's definitely not a great time of year, Bert,' Georgina said with a sigh, and messaged Sybbie, Jodie and Francesca in case they'd missed the text from the teacher.

> No class tonight. Just as well – Bert stole six
> sausage rolls from the back of the car, so I'm glad
> I can stay in to keep an eye on him. G x

As she'd half expected, Sybbie messaged straight back with,

> Max and Jet would have done the same. Dogs!
> S x

Georgina continued with her work until Colin arrived back from work. But that evening Bert didn't leap up to greet Colin with delirious tail wags, the way he usually did.

'Is Bert all right?' Colin asked.

'Not really. He's digesting illicit sausage rolls,' she said. 'We went to see Valerie Waring this afternoon, and I took her a couple of Louise's spicy sausage rolls as a treat. And I bought half a dozen chicken ones for you to take into the office tomorrow, but stupidly

I left them just within Bert's reach – you can guess what happened.'

'Ah. So the sausage rolls are no more,' Colin said.

Bert gave a gentle moan.

'Hopefully he'll sleep it off,' Georgina said. 'Pilates is cancelled tonight, luckily – the poor teacher's gone down with a bug. I'd rather keep an eye on Bert.'

Later that evening, Bert threw up over the rug in the living room. Colin offered to grab the disinfectant and clear up while Georgina took the dog outside.

A couple of minutes later, she came back into the kitchen to grab her car keys. 'I've just called the vet, who says to bring him straight in,' she said. She didn't care that it would be an expensive visit, being after hours; the dog was way more important to her than money. 'Bert's poo was very loose – which I kind of expected, given that he'd just been sick – but there was blood in it.'

And he'd eaten six of Louise's sausage rolls.

Only a few days ago, a whole class of nine-year-olds had become ill after eating sausage rolls at Great Wenborough Mill. Their teacher had died.

Had the sausage rolls made Bert ill, too?

And, more worryingly, would he recover?

SIX

'We'll take my car and I'll drive us to the vet's,' Colin said, 'so you can sit in the back with Bert and comfort him.'

Colin had only picked up his new car last week. Bert was likely to have another episode of diarrhoea or sickness on the way to the vet. Georgina bit her lip. 'But what if he's i—'

'I really don't care about the car,' Colin cut in. 'It's not important. Bert comes first. We need to get him to the vet as quickly as possible and keep him comfortable on the way. We'll put a blanket down on the back seat; if he's sick again before we get there and I need to get the car valeted tomorrow, so be it.'

She should have realised Colin wouldn't make a fuss about his new car. A few months back, when he'd rushed her to hospital and she'd worried about making a mess in his car, he'd said much the same thing. His priorities – putting Bert first – were definitely ones she agreed with.

'Does the vet need you to take a sample of his poo?' Colin asked.

'I didn't think to check,' Georgina admitted. The fact that Bert was so poorly had shoved everything but sheer panic out of her mind. 'But yes, that's probably a good idea.'

'Give me a jar or something and tell me roughly where he went to the loo, and I'll sort it out while you get him in his harness and in the car,' Colin said.

Gratefully, Georgina found him a clean lidded jar and gave him directions, and Colin headed out to the back garden armed with the torch on his phone and the jar, plus a pair of the latex gloves that were always in his pocket. Meanwhile she put an old sheet down in the back of Colin's car, then gently picked Bert up and laid him on the back seat, clicking his harness into the seatbelt.

Colin locked the kitchen door, then drove them to the vet. 'He'll be all right, Georgie,' he said, clearly trying to reassure her.

Georgina wasn't so sure. Bert looked so poorly. 'Mmm,' she said, not having the headspace to argue.

Colin didn't make her chatter on the way; he simply tuned the radio to a station playing something soothing and classical.

What had made Bert ill so suddenly?

Could it have been the sausage rolls? But if it was a simple matter of eating too much rich food, surely the dog would have started to feel better as soon as he'd been sick? Or he would have been a bit gassy, as he usually was after a bowlful of roast dinner on Christmas Day. The presence of blood in the diarrhoea really worried her.

'It's going to be all right, boy,' she said, echoing Colin's words as she stroked the top of the spaniel's head. Though she didn't believe a word she was saying. Worry churned through her stomach and she had to choke back the tears.

'I'll carry him in,' Colin said, handing her the car keys when he'd parked. 'The poo sample's on the floor in the passenger side.'

Once Colin had lifted Bert out of the car, she took the jar from the front of the car, then clicked the key fob to lock the door. The vet – David Glass, a man in his early sixties with neat grey hair and a calm, practical manner that Georgina appreciated – was waiting for them in the practice's reception area, and Colin carried the spaniel into the consulting room and set him down gently on the stainless-steel table.

'We brought a sample of his poo with us. Sorry, the vomit was already contaminated with cleaning stuff, so we didn't bring that,' Colin said.

'The stool sample's helpful,' David said. 'I'll get it tested.' He examined Bert. 'The poor little lad's clearly feeling rough,' he said. 'Can you tell me, Georgie, has he drunk from a pond or a ditch in the last couple of days, or eaten anything he shouldn't have? I've got spaniels myself, so I know what they're like – they'll find something that's been decaying for days in the fields, and take a sneaky chomp.'

'We haven't been anywhere near a pond or ditch. He's only drunk fresh water from his own bowl, or at Sybbie's, and her dogs are both fine,' Georgina said. 'He did scoff six chicken sausage rolls in the back of the car that he wasn't supposed to have this afternoon. I thought the pastry would probably be too rich for him, so I wasn't surprised when he threw up. But then he wanted to go outside and I noticed his poo was really loose – and there was blood in it.'

'My grandson was ill from eating a sausage roll earlier this week,' David said, frowning. 'My daughter said he'd been on a school trip to Great Wenborough Mill, and the whole class started being sick. I thought it was a bit odd, because the winter vomiting bug wouldn't work that quickly on an entire class. I suggested it was probably something they all ate – I remember going on a school trip to the chocolate factory in Norwich when I was a kid, and we all ate so much on the tour that we were all sick in the coach on the way home – and she said something about sausage rolls.'

Georgina swallowed hard. 'I know about that. My friend's son was in the same class, and I gave him and his mum a lift home.' She'd wanted to support Louise, but now she really, really regretted buying the sausage rolls. Why hadn't she just bought lemon cake from the farm shop, like she normally did?

'To be fair to Louise Wilkins,' Colin said, 'I've been investigating the incident. The council's hygiene team went to the mill and they couldn't find a problem.'

But all the children in Harry's class *had* been ill after eating sausage rolls at the mill. Miss Hurst had died after eating a sausage roll at the mill. And although Georgina and Sybbie had both been absolutely fine after eating a sausage roll from the mill the following day, Bert was very far from fine now after eating several of Louise's sausage rolls. If he hadn't scoffed them, Georgie would have given them to Colin and his team – and it was looking very likely that Colin, Mo and Larissa would have become ill too.

And then, as if her thoughts were slowly marshalling themselves through the panic she felt over Bert, a seriously nasty thought struck her. 'Colin, I gave two of the sausage rolls to Valerie Waring. Not the same type as the ones I bought for you – the ones that Bert stole – but...' She stared at him. 'I think I ought to check on her.'

'I remember Valerie bringing Bert here for his first vaccinations. She moved into the sheltered housing place, didn't she?' David asked, still examining Bert. 'I believe they have a warden there twenty-four seven. They might be able to check on her for you.'

'She's probably fine,' Georgina said, not feeling at all convinced by her own words, 'but, given that she's not in the best of health, I'd rather make a nuisance of myself and call her to make sure she's all right.'

'I'm going to keep Bert here overnight,' David said, 'and I'll put him on a drip so we can get some fluids into him. We'll keep a close eye on him, and I'll let you know how he's doing in the morning. Once we've got that sample analysed, I'll have a better idea of what's causing the sickness and how to treat him. There is a canine vomiting virus going round at the moment – I've had a couple of elderly dogs in who were quite poorly with it, but they responded well to treatment, and Bert's younger and stronger than they were, so if it's that I think he'll be fine.' He patted Georgina's arm. 'I would say try not to worry, but I know that's not really possible when your pet's unwell. But I promise you we'll look after him.'

Colin stroked Bert's head. 'You concentrate on getting better, lovely boy. Remember we love you.'

Georgina choked back a sob as she said goodbye to Bert. Please don't let this be the last goodbye. She was far from ready to lose him. Bert gave the tiniest wag of his tail, as if to reassure her that he planned to get well enough for her to take him home again very soon.

She didn't quite make it to the car when she burst into racking sobs.

Colin wrapped his arms round her and held her close. 'Hey. David's good at his job. He's going to get fluids into Bert to keep him going until the lab results are back. I know you're scared that Bert's not coming home again, Georgie, but you're not going to lose him, I promise.'

But that wasn't something Colin *could* promise, Georgina thought. What if there really had been some kind of poison in the sausage rolls? How long would it take to identify it? What if it was too late to reverse any damage that had been done to Bert's system by the poison? 'I wish I'd never bought those bloody sausage rolls,' she said.

'It wasn't your fault, Georgie. You weren't to know. The hygiene team had given Louise the green light.' He frowned. 'I'm going to get to the bottom of this, I swear to you. If there's a poisoner in the village, I'll find them, and I'll bring them to justice.'

Now *that* was something she could believe. And Colin was good at his job. He meant it. She dragged in a breath. 'Sorry. It's just – *Bert...*'

'I know. I love him, too. He's a beautiful boy. And he's still in his prime. We'll have him home with us again. Really soon,' Colin reassured her.

She nodded. 'I'd better check on Valerie.'

But Valerie didn't answer the phone.

'She might be asleep,' Colin said, 'but I understand why you're worried. Let's go and see her.'

When they got to the sheltered complex, Valerie didn't answer her door, either. Colin took Georgina's hand; together they found the warden's house and knocked on the door.

'It's a bit late,' the warden said when she opened the door. 'Not really an appropriate time to visit any of our residents.'

'Just to reassure you,' Colin said, and showed her his warrant card.

'The police?' Her eyes widened. 'Is there a problem?'

'There might be,' Colin said, 'though I'm not here in an official capacity. We're concerned about one of your residents, Valerie Waring.'

Georgina explained about the sausage rolls she'd brought round to Valerie that afternoon, and her suspicion that there might be something wrong with them. 'Just now, we couldn't get Valerie to answer her phone, so we came to her flat. There aren't any lights on and she's not answering the door. I'm probably being paranoid, but I'd much rather look stupid and need to apologise to her for asking you to wake her from a deep sleep, than for something to have happened to her and not doing anything about it.'

The warden was already putting on her shoes and put a bunch of keys in her bag. 'Was she all right when you left this afternoon?'

'Of course she was,' Georgina said, slightly nettled. 'I wouldn't have just abandoned her if she was ill. At the very least I would have come to the office and let you know she wasn't well.'

'Sorry. I didn't mean to imply anything,' the warden said. 'Hopefully this is all just a misunderstanding. But with you telling me your dog was taken ill tonight after eating the sausage rolls, I'm inclined to agree with you. It's better to be safe than sorry.'

'My dog was Valerie's dog originally – I bring him over to see her every few weeks,' Georgina said. 'Please don't tell her that he's ill, because I don't want her to worry.'

'All right,' the warden agreed.

Valerie still didn't answer the door. When the warden unlocked the front door and called Valerie's name, there was no answer. Finally, when she walked further into the flat, using the torch on her phone to light the way, they heard a weak groan coming from the direction of the bedroom. And there was a sour smell that reminded Georgina of the way Harry had vomited in the back of her car, a few days before.

The warden switched on the light in the bedroom; Georgina could hear the low hum of voices but couldn't quite make out the words. Then the warden called, 'Can you ring for an ambulance? Tell them she's eighty, she has a temperature and she's been sick, and she has stomach cramps. I'm going to try to get her more comfortable and clean her up a bit before they arrive.'

'Is there anything else we can do to help?' Georgina asked as Colin rang the emergency services.

'Just wait outside so they can see you and know where to come,' the warden said.

It was only a matter of minutes, but it felt a lot longer than that when the ambulance turned up. Georgina explained about the sausage rolls, and what had happened to Bert. 'But please don't tell her that Bert's ill. Bert used to be her dog, and she rehomed him with me when she came here,' she added urgently in an undertone.

The paramedics brought Valerie out on a trolley.

'I'm so sorry, Valerie,' Georgina said as they loaded Valerie onto the ambulance.

'It's not your fault, love,' Valerie said, her voice raspy.

Oh, but it was. Because she'd bought the sausage roll that had made Valerie ill.

'Will you let me know when there's any news, please?' she asked the warden.

'I'm afraid I can't, as you're not her next of kin,' the warden said.

'Sometimes,' Georgina said, 'it's better to do the kind thing than the regulatory thing.' If the warden wouldn't help, she'd go to the hospital herself tomorrow.

The warden looked at her, then sighed. 'In your shoes, I'd feel the same. All right. Just don't tell anyone that I've breached confidentiality.'

'I won't,' Georgina promised. 'Thank you.' She gave the

warden her business card. 'I don't mind whether you contact me by voicemail, email, text – just please let me know as soon as you hear something.'

Unlocking the kitchen door and not seeing Bert's usual ecstatic, wiggly, tail-wagging welcome made Georgina feel even worse.

'Georgie. I know you're worried sick. I'll sit with Bert tonight and I'll check in with you in the morning,' Doris said.

It was enough to make the tears spill over again. Luckily Colin didn't ask her why, because she didn't want to risk a fight by telling him.

Knowing that Bert wasn't going to be alone – and he'd know that Doris was there with him – was a comfort, but Georgina still slept badly. So did Colin.

'I'm glad I don't have any guests booked in to the barn this week,' Georgina said when she managed to drag herself out of bed. 'I don't think I could face them.'

'Understandably,' Colin said. He climbed out of bed, too, wrapped his arms round her and held her close. 'It's going to be all right, Georgie.'

She wasn't so sure. She was dreading going downstairs to the empty kitchen, especially because Doris hadn't checked in yet. Was that because Bert was worse – or the unthinkable had happened, and Doris couldn't bring herself to break the news?

The reality, when Georgina finally made herself walk into the kitchen and fill the kettle, was even worse than she'd imagined. 'The house just doesn't feel right without Bert,' she said, going through the motions of making coffee. 'It's too empty.'

'Nobody waiting patiently for the last bite of toast,' Colin said with a sigh.

'He's going to be all right,' Doris said.

Georgina started; she hadn't realised that Doris was there.

'They're going to ring you this morning and tell you they'll keep him in for a bit longer, but he's on the mend,' Doris continued. 'I kept telling him how much you love him, and I stayed with him all night until the vet nurse came in this morning and checked him over.'

Georgina blinked to signify that she'd heard. It was a relief to know that Bert was going to recover – and that Doris had been kind enough to keep him company – but he still wasn't quite out of the woods.

'I know you can't talk to me while Colin is here,' Doris said, acknowledging both Georgina's blink and the reason for it. 'I'll be back later.'

'I've been thinking,' Colin said, crumbling the toast crust on his plate. 'You said the sausage rolls you bought for Valerie weren't the same as the ones Bert ate.'

'No,' Georgina said. 'They were spicy chicken ones. Valerie likes spicy food. The ones Bert ate were chicken and herb.'

'I very much doubt that someone adulterated them in the shop just for you alone,' Colin said, looking thoughtful. 'I think whoever's behind this is doing this randomly – trying to affect as many people as possible rather than focusing on select customers.'

'Louise was the one who served me,' Georgina said. 'I saw her hands the whole time. I didn't see her add anything to the sausage rolls.'

'I think it's more likely that the whole batch was contaminated, maybe even before they were cooked,' he said. 'Which means that anyone who bought something from the bakery yesterday might have been affected, too. Your Pilates teacher – did you say she'd gone down with a bug?'

'That's why she cancelled the class last night,' Georgina said.

'What if,' Colin asked, 'she'd eaten a sausage roll from Mill Bakery?'

Georgina stared at him, horrified. 'Oh, no. That didn't even occur to me.'

'It's a possibility,' he said. 'Are you in the village social media group?'

'Yes, but I don't bother looking at it much,' she said. 'It's full of people moaning about roadworks, other people's parking, noisy kids, dog walkers not picking up their dogs' poo, and people having bonfires without warning their neighbours.'

'So it's the most likely place for people to complain if they think they've been made ill by something they've bought locally?' he checked.

'I guess,' Georgina said. And then she twigged. 'People who are going to say they bought sausage rolls from Mill Bakery and were made ill.'

He nodded. 'Would you mind logging in and taking a look for me?'

She did so, and grimaced. 'There are half a dozen posts from people complaining of a stomachache, having an upset stomach or throwing up. And they're all talking about Louise's sausage rolls. Some of them are asking if it was her fault or if it was the meat she bought from Billy.'

'My theory is that we have a poisoner in our midst,' Colin said. 'Right now, I don't know who, and I don't know why they're picking on Louise or Billy. But we need this to stop before someone eats a fatal dose.'

'Not necessarily a person.' Her dog wasn't out of the woods, yet. Even though she trusted Doris, she really needed to hear the words out loud from the vet. Georgina logged off. 'I'm going to ring the vet and see how Bert is.'

It took her four tries before she got past the answering machine and the receptionist actually answered. They wanted to keep Bert at the surgery for the rest of the day; he still wasn't eating, he wasn't drinking, and they were keeping him on a drip.

Exactly what Doris had told her, but it was still upsetting to have confirmation that he wasn't properly better yet. 'I hate this,' Georgina said. 'I feel so helpless. There's nothing at all I can do to help him, and it doesn't sit right with me.'

'Is Sybbie free today? Even if you end up just following her round the garden, twitching out whatever weeds grow at this time of year, it'd be better than you being here on your own all day,' Colin said.

'I'll check,' Georgina said, and sent Sybbie a text to let her know what was going on.

Sybbie rang her immediately. 'Come straight over, dear girl. Why didn't you ring me last night? You must be beside yourself. When Max had to have a couple of teeth out, I was in bits, so you must be in a terrible state right now.'

'I am,' Georgina admitted. 'Thank you. I'll come over now. And it gets worse, Sybbie. I took Valerie Waring a couple of sausage rolls yesterday afternoon, and she's in hospital.'

'Oh, no. Actually, *don't* drive to me – I'll pick you up,' Sybbie said. 'I'll be with you in ten minutes.'

Georgina texted Jodie to let her know not to come – they'd finished the deep cleaning of Rookery Barn over the last couple of days and there were no guests to prep for. She also told Jodie about Bert and Valerie.

Jodie rang her immediately. 'I can borrow Mike's car and come over, if you need me.'

'That's kind, but I'm going to Sybbie's,' Georgina said.

'All right. As long as you're not going to be on your own. And please will you keep me posted about how Valerie and Bert are?'

'Of course I will,' Georgina promised.

Colin waited until Sybbie arrived before he left for work. 'Call me if you hear anything from the vet or the warden,' he said to Georgina. 'And I'll let you know if I hear anything.'

Sybbie took Georgina back to Little Wenborough Manor and made a fuss of her, but Georgina couldn't settle. It didn't feel right being there without Bert. Max and Jet stayed close to her, as if trying to comfort her, but it wasn't enough.

Colin texted her in the middle of the morning.

> Doctor's surgery confirms several ill after eating
> sausage rolls. Hospital says same.

'It really does look as if someone is targeting either Louise's business or Billy's,' Sybbie remarked. 'But who's behind it? And why?'

'I don't know,' Georgina said, 'but right now I'd like to eviscerate them with a rusty spoon for what they've done.'

Sybbie winced, but nodded. 'Me, too.'

In the middle of the morning, Colin called in to the manor house.

Georgina hadn't expected to see him, and was instantly worried. 'Has something happened?'

'Not with Bert, as far as I know,' he said, clearly second-guessing her immediate panic, 'but yes. Have you heard anything from the vet, yet?'

She shook her head. 'Should I have done?'

'We've got Miss Hurst's lab tests back from Sammy Granger,' he said grimly. 'I've already called the vet to let him know the results, in case it changes the treatment for Bert.'

Bile rose in Georgina's throat and her stomach twisted. This sounded like bad news. 'What did the tests find?'

'Miss Hurst died from ingesting poison.' Colin looked very sombre. 'Rat poison.'

SEVEN

'Oh, my God.' Georgina found herself tensing with shock. 'Are you telling me Bert ate sausage rolls laced with *rat poison?*'

'Possibly,' Colin said. 'We won't know for definite until we've run tests. David says there's no real change in his condition, so let's take that as a win for now. Bert hasn't deteriorated. That's a good sign.'

Or was it?

Rat poison.

Bert, like most spaniels and Labradors, was greedy. He'd eaten six of the sausage rolls. What if they'd all been laced with the rat poison? What did that do to the body? Would it affect his heart? His breathing? Would it affect dogs more than humans? Georgina couldn't think straight; and she was too shocked and upset by the news to form any coherent questions or take in any answers.

'I'm going to collect the sausage rolls from the bakery now, including any from yesterday that have been thrown away,' Colin said.

Wasn't that more of a junior officer's task than a DI's? As if the question showed on her face, Colin said, 'I would have asked Larissa to do it, but I wanted to see you and tell you this face-to-face. I didn't want you to mishear anything in a phone call.'

She was touched that he'd remembered her difficulty with phones; even though her hearing aids connected to her phone so she didn't have to rely on a speakerphone anymore, she still struggled with calls sometimes.

'I'm also picking up all the chicken and sausages from Billy's butchery,' he added. 'Any customers need to be contacted urgently to make sure they don't eat the potentially poisoned goods, and we're asking them to return everything to Billy. We'll do another pickup later. We know which particular poison killed Miss Hurst, so we'll have to work with that as the basis of treatment for anyone who's been affected until we know more. I've let the hospital and the doctor's surgery know, as well as the vet – not just for Bert, but other pets might also have been given a bit of sausage roll as a treat and ended up at the vet's.'

'How did rat poison get into the sausage rolls in the first place?' Sybbie asked. 'And it's odd that the children recovered remarkably quickly whereas Miss Hurst died. Did she have more poison in her sausage roll than they did?'

'We really don't know,' Colin said. 'Louise said she threw everything out after the school trip, and the bins from the bakery were collected the next day, so there's no evidence available from Monday's batches for testing. I'm hoping that somebody who bought sausage rolls yesterday might not have eaten them, so there's something we can test.'

'Valerie Waring,' Georgina said. 'I bought her two sausage rolls. She might have put one of them in her fridge, saving it for today.'

'Good point,' he said. 'I'll ask the warden to let me into the flat so I can check and take the evidence, if necessary.' He gave her a hug, and patted Sybbie's shoulder. 'I know neither of you will say anything to anyone about what I've just told you, because you both know this is all confidential.'

Strictly speaking, he shouldn't have discussed the case with them at all, Georgina knew, but he'd clearly wanted to keep her in the picture about Bert. She was glad he'd told her, even though she was even more worried now. She'd rather be prepared for the worst than to have it hit her as a complete out-of-the-blue shock.

'And try not to worry about Bert, Georgie,' Colin added. 'He's still holding his own.'

Sybbie kept Georgina busy in the greenhouse for the rest of the morning; Sybbie suggested looking into Margaret's case some more, but Georgina couldn't concentrate – not until she knew that Bert was going to make a proper recovery.

Finally the vet rang Georgina at lunchtime. 'The lab managed to do a rapid test and the results are back. You'll be pleased to know it's not rat poison, like DI Bradshaw suspected.'

'It's not?' Georgina's knees sagged in relief and she had to sit down.

'It's campylobacter – a bacterial infection,' David said. 'You told me Bert hadn't drunk water from a pond or a ditch, so he must have contracted it from contaminated food.'

'Do you think the chicken sausage rolls were the source of the campylobacter?' Georgina asked.

'It's the most likely source,' David confirmed. 'Unless you gave Bert any raw poultry, this week?'

'No,' she confirmed.

'The good news is that it's a self-limiting condition, and he should be back to normal over the next couple of days,' David said. 'I'm going to give him a short course of antibiotics, and you can take him back home this afternoon if you're happy to give him a bland diet and make sure he takes the antibiotics.'

'I'm very happy to do that,' Georgina said. A tear brimmed over her lashes. 'I'm just so glad Bert can come home.' Her voice was shaky with relief.

'He's a bit brighter than he was, but I'd still like you to bring him back on Monday so we can see how he's getting on, and I might give you some probiotics for him after he's finished the antibiotics,' David said. 'Remember that campylobacter can be transmitted to humans, so you need to be really strict about hand hygiene over the next week or so until it's completely through his system.'

'Campylobacter,' Georgina mused. 'The symptoms are sickness and diarrhoea, abdominal pain and fever, right?'

'Pretty much,' David said.

Which matched Valerie Waring's symptoms.

So maybe it wasn't rat poison that had made her ill. Maybe it was campylobacter. And maybe Valerie, like Bert, would recover well, rather than dying like Miss Hurst had. Georgina could only hope.

'I'll see you very soon,' she said. She ended the call and hugged Sybbie. 'Bert's going to be all right, and I can go and get him now.'

'So I gathered. Campylobacter can be nasty,' Sybbie said. 'Poor boy. But I'm so glad it's not rat poison. I wonder where he picked it up?'

'It could have been the sausage rolls. Maybe the chicken wasn't cooked properly?'

'I can't see Louise making a rookie mistake like that,' Sybbie said. 'But I'm glad that it was something that seems accidental rather than someone deliberately lacing the food with rat poison. I can't get my head around that.'

'I'd better tell Colin. And then could I ask you a huge favour – would you drop me home so I can go and collect Bert, please?' Georgina asked.

'Better than that,' Sybbie said, 'I'll drive you to the vet and then drop both of you home. It'll save time and it means you'll see Bert faster.' She gave Georgina a sympathetic smile. 'I'd be as much of a basket case as you if it was Max or Jet who was ill, and in your shoes I'd want them home as fast as possible. We'll go now, and you can ring Colin on the way.'

'Thank you,' Georgina said gratefully.

'I'm so glad Bert's going to be all right,' Colin said when she rang him and told him the news. 'And you're absolutely sure it wasn't brodifacoum – the rat poison that killed Miss Hurst – that made him ill? It was definitely campylobacter?'

'That's what David said,' Georgina confirmed.

'I've got Valerie's second sausage roll. Your guess was right; she'd put it in the fridge. I'll get it tested for campylobacter as well as rat poison, and I'll do the same for the rest of the food I picked up,' Colin said. He paused. 'According to the website I'm reading right now, the most common cause of transmission for campylobacter is contaminated food. Uncooked meat, using chopping boards for raw and cooked foods, bird feeders – and an infected person could contaminate food through poor hand hygiene. It also says it's usually a couple of days before people start to feel ill, so something's odd here. The children and Valerie – and Bert, for that matter – all went down with it very quickly.'

'Do you think it was campylobacter or rat poison that made the children and Valerie ill?' Georgina asked.

'Until we get the test results for the sausage rolls back, I don't know,' Colin said. 'Plus we don't have samples for the children.'

'Maybe whoever's behind the poisoning used a combination of both,' Georgina suggested. 'And perhaps the children were more vulnerable to it because their immune systems aren't as strong as an adult's. Valerie was frail to start with, too, so maybe that's why she reacted so badly.' She bit her lip. 'I really hope Valerie pulls through.'

'I'll call the hospital and the doctor's surgery now, and let them know the latest,' Colin promised. 'And I'll try to be back as soon as I can this evening.'

'All right,' she said. 'I'll see you later.'

At the vet's, Georgina had a joyful reunion with Bert, and Sybbie stayed at the farmhouse with them both for a while to help Bert settle back in. Georgina messaged Jodie to let her know that Bert was home, and got the reply, *AMAZING! Let me no if u need anything x*

'I was so terrified he wasn't coming home,' Georgina said.

'I loathe the expression "fur children",' Sybbie said, 'but it's true, isn't it? We really do love them as if they're our children. I'm lucky, because Giles' – her son – 'lives next door, but it's hard for you with your two living hours away.'

They'd been back at the farmhouse for half an hour when the doorbell rang – clearly someone who hadn't been here before, Georgina thought, because her family and friends knew to come straight round to the kitchen door rather than bother with the front door.

Louise stood on the doorstep with a bunch of flowers. 'I brought you these,' she said awkwardly. 'I'm so sorry Bert has been ill because of my sausage rolls. How's he doing?'

'Come and see for yourself,' Georgina said with a smile, hoping that it would make Louise feel more at ease, and ushered her through to the kitchen.

Bert gave a half-hearted wag of his tail, but didn't move from his bed, the way he usually would.

'Hello, Louise,' Sybbie said with a smile. 'Good to see you.'

'She came round with these lovely flowers and to see how Bert was,' Georgina said, taking a vase from under the sink and putting the flowers in water.

'I don't even dare touch him in case I'm the one who's contaminating everything without knowing it,' Louise said. 'The sausage rolls on Monday and yesterday. I don't...' Her face crumpled for a moment. 'I just don't understand what's going on. I've always been meticulous about food safety and cross-contamination. I made sure my staff were properly trained and knew what to do. I've never, ever had anything like this happen before – not when I worked in London, and not since I opened the mill and the bakery here.'

'I imagine Billy's just as shocked as you are,' Sybbie said dryly.

'Billy's done nothing wrong, either,' Louise said. 'Someone has to be tampering with the food, doing something that contaminates it with campylobacter or...' She closed her eyes. 'That poor teacher. Rat poison. DI Bradshaw said it was that that killed her. Brodifacoum. But who would put rat poison in food, knowing that someone would eat it and at the very least be ill, and at the worst die?'

'I think Louise is being framed,' Doris said. 'Just like Margaret was. She's being blamed for poison when she's not responsible for it. If we can find out what really happened to Margaret, it might help us work out who's framing Louise.'

'Sit down and have a cup of tea with us,' Georgina offered.

Louise's face was pinched. 'That's kind of you, but I need to get back to the mill,' she said wearily. 'I've left Annie in charge of the kids so Hugo can at least work from home – he came back from London, just after you and Sybbie came for the tour. I think Marion nagged him into it. She's been the one giving me moral support, and I'm ridiculously grateful for it bec—' She stopped abruptly and grimaced. 'Never mind. I won't bother you with my troubles.'

'It sounds to me,' Georgina said, 'as if you really could do with that cup of tea and someone to listen. And it's not going any further than Sybbie or me.' She persuaded Louise to sit down at the table with Sybbie while she put the kettle on. Bert dragged himself out of bed to sit by Louise and put his chin briefly on her knee in a gesture of comfort, before curling up and resting his chin on her feet.

'Lovely boy,' Louise said softly, and made a fuss of him.

She accepted the cup of tea gratefully. 'I don't feel as if I deserve this, but thank you.'

'Of course you deserve it,' Sybbie said.

'Everyone in Great Wenborough and Little Wenborough is going to think of me as the poison lady now. Not the person who restored the mill from dereliction and tried to be part of the community, but the incomer from London who made a whole class of children sick – and now what looks like half of Great Wenborough and Little Wenborough as well,' Louise said miserably.

'No, they're not,' Sybbie said. 'Anyone who really knows you will know it's not your fault. Georgie and I will help to clear your name.'

'But how? This is a serious breach of health and safety regulations. The hygiene team have already been in and cleared me, but they're coming back now to do another investigation,' Louise said. 'Even if they clear me a second time, people are going to talk, and mud sticks. I'm not sure the business is going to survive.'

'Ask her if anyone's tried to buy the place,' Doris said.

Georgina frowned slightly to signal that she'd heard. 'This is a weird question, Louise, but has anyone made an offer to buy you out recently – I mean the mill and the bakery?'

'No,' Louise said, looking puzzled. 'Why?'

'Just a thought,' Georgina said. 'Actually Cesca said there were some rumours about a murder linked to the mill, back in the day. Sybbie and I thought it was probably a mix-up with some of the old murder ballads, but we've had a look in the archives, and it seems that the daughter of the miller in Great Wenborough really was convicted of murder, back in 1845.'

Louise's eyes widened in horror. 'I had no idea! Oh, my God.' She put a hand to her mouth. 'That's awful. And, actually, it makes me feel as if the mill is cursed.'

'I know how that feels,' Sybbie said sympathetically. 'Last year, we found there was a mystery at the manor, involving Bernard's ancestors. One of the archaeologists disappeared during the Victorian dig at the Roman Baths – and one of the present-day archaeologists died at the modern dig.'

'I remember reading about that in the paper,' Louise said. 'It must have been awful for you.'

'Georgie and I, with a bit of help' – Sybbie glanced just beyond Georgina's shoulder, to acknowledge Doris's part – 'did some research and found out what happened. We think there was possibly a miscarriage of justice at the mill and Margaret Chorley – that's the miller's daughter – might not have done what she was accused of. Just as you haven't done anything wrong.'

'Do you know what really happened to Margaret?' Louise asked.

'We've just started looking into it,' Georgina said. 'Though I've been too worried about Bert to do much else.'

'Of course.' Louise's face tightened. 'I'm so sorry again that he's been ill.'

'It wasn't your fault,' Georgina said.

'It feels like it was.' Louise sighed. 'I've been so caught up in the restoration and building up the business that I've kind of neglected everything else. Hugo is right. We should never have come here. We should have stayed in London.'

Georgina and Sybbie exchanged a glance. Louise had said she was grateful for her mother-in-law's moral support but then broke off the subject; it sounded as if her husband really wasn't giving her the support she needed.

'You mentioned the other day that Hugo stays in London for most of the week,' Sybbie said.

'He does now,' Louise said. 'The commute's too much. It's half an hour from here to the station, the best part of two hours on the train, and then more travelling the other end.'

'That's a lot,' Georgina said.

Louise nodded. 'We came to Norfolk on holiday when Sam was small, and we loved it here. The slower pace of life, the way people seem to have time for each other like they don't in London... And London was just horrible during lockdown. When we saw the mill was for sale, together with its cottage, it felt like a sign we should change all our lives and move here. Sam was young enough to cope with moving schools, Noah was a toddler and there was space in the village preschool for him, and I wasn't yet pregnant with Isla. We'd hired Annie to help with the children, and Hugo said he'd had enough of the city and he'd be happy to work from home.' She sighed. 'But finance is such a fast-moving, high-powered job. I should have guessed he'd miss the life we had back in London. It was all right at first, but then he started getting more and more miserable. He says Norfolk's great for a holiday but he just can't live here all the time. So we came to a compromise where he spends the weekdays in London – he's got a tiny flat there – and he comes home for the weekend.'

'It's hard to juggle family life and a business,' Georgina said.

'Isn't it just? We're lucky to have Annie, even though she can be hard work at times,' Louise said. 'Though, once Isla's at school full-time, I have a feeling she'll move back to London. There's not really enough going on in the village for her.'

Georgina remembered Jodie saying that the nanny didn't mix at the school gates. Maybe that was why, because she wasn't happy here and didn't feel like she fitted in.

Louise finished her tea. 'I'm sorry. I've taken up your afternoon, moaning about my woes, when you've got Bert to worry about. And I ought to be getting back.'

'Don't apologise,' Georgina said. 'It probably did you good to get that off your chest.'

'It did. Thank you.' Louise gave her a rueful smile. 'Now I just have to pick myself up again, dust myself down, and try to get my business back on track.'

Sybbie had just gone back to the Manor when Georgina's phone beeped with a text from Will, her son. *Hey, Mum. Can I come home for a few days?*

Of course you can, she texted back. *Just let me know roughly when you'll be here so I can make sure I have dinner for you x*

Be with you by about seven tonight, traffic permitting, if that's OK, he messaged.

She frowned. This wasn't usual for Will. He normally liked to plan things weeks in advance. And to be here in Norfolk for seven o'clock, it meant he was going to leave in the next two minutes. It sounded almost as if he were running away from something. *Everything OK?* she checked.

Sure. See you soon x, he messaged.

She glanced at her watch. Her daughter, an actor who lived in

London, would be out of rehearsals at the Regency Theatre in Islington by now, with any luck.

Got a minute for a quick chat? she texted.

A minute later, her phone rang. 'Mum? Is everything all right?' Bea asked. 'Or are you in the middle of a case and want some help?'

'A bit of both, really,' she said. She filled Bea in on what had happened with Bert.

'Oh, my God! Why didn't you tell me yesterday? I would have come home,' Bea said.

Georgina was grateful that both her children considered Rookery Farm their home, even though neither of them had grown up there or lived there, and Stephen – their father – had died the year before she decided to move here. Or maybe it was a case of them feeling that their mum was where home was. Bea had sent her a Mother's Day card last year along those lines, and it had made her tear up. 'I know, love, but I also know you're busy with work, and there was nothing anyone apart from the vet could do. He's on the mend now.'

'Hmm. So what about the case?'

'The place where I bought the sausage rolls is connected to a murder in the nineteenth century,' Georgina explained. 'But Doris says that Margaret – the woman who was accused of the murder and hanged for it – didn't do it. I've got a broadside and the newspaper reports, so I'll be working through those over the next few days.' She paused. 'But what I really wanted to know was if you've spoken to Will, recently?'

'Not really,' Bea admitted, sounding faintly guilty. 'We've both been busy. Why?'

'He's asked if he can come home for a few days.'

'And your maternal sixth sense makes you think there's more to it?' Bea asked.

'My maternal sixth sense, as you put it, can usually tell if something's not right,' Georgina reminded her.

'He hasn't mentioned anything to me,' Bea said. 'Mum, if he's not all right – let me know, and I'll come home. I'm off on Sunday. I was supposed to be going out with friends, but Will's more important. I can move things round if I have to.'

How proud Stephen would be of the close-knit, caring children he'd left behind. Just as she was. 'Thanks, love,' Georgina said. 'I'll keep you posted.'

Between worrying about Will and worrying about Bert, Georgina didn't make much headway with working on the newspaper reports about Margaret's trial. In the end, she gave up and started to chop some chicken and chorizo for a jambalaya-based dish that was one of her son's favourites. 'You can have some plain cooked chicken and plain rice,' she told Bert. 'And none of it's going to be raw.'

Bert watched her from his bed in the kitchen, still subdued; normally he sat as close to her as possible when she cooked, in the hope of titbits coming his way.

Colin came home early and made a fuss of Bert. 'It's good to see that tail wagging,' he said. Then he sniffed. 'Something smells good.'

'Sort-of jambalaya,' she said. 'I'm just letting the flavours develop and then I'll reheat it for dinner. Will's coming home tonight.'

'Because he's worried about Bert – and about how *you* are?' Colin asked.

She shook her head. 'He doesn't know about Bert, yet. I think something's up. But I guess he'll tell me when he's ready.'

'Do you want me to go back to Norwich, and give you both some space?' Colin asked.

'No, it's fine. Though maybe later this evening you could take Bert for a very, very short s-t-r-o-l-l, or something, to give us a few minutes alone?'

'Of course,' Colin said.

'Louise Wilkins popped over this afternoon with some flowers, and to see how Bert was doing,' Georgina said.

'That was kind of her.'

But there was something oddly flat with Colin's tone. 'Is every-thing all right?' she asked.

'Not really.' He blew out a breath. 'I don't know how to tell you this.'

'Tell me what? You're scaring me,' she warned.

He wrapped his arms round her. 'I'm so sorry, Georgie. There isn't a nice way to say it. I can't pretty it up, so I'll have to be blunt. The hospital called.' He took a deep breath. 'Valerie didn't make it.'

EIGHT

Georgina stared at him, too horrified at first to say a word.

Valerie Waring was *dead*?

'Oh, my God,' she said, her voice scratchy with shock. And then she swallowed hard. 'That's terrible. Poor Valerie.' She rubbed a hand over her eyes. 'It's my fault. I don't think I'll ever forgive myself for taking her those sausage rolls.'

'You can't blame yourself, Georgie. The bakery at the mill had been cleared by the local food hygiene team and you bought those sausage rolls in good faith. As soon as Bert was ill and you realised there might be a problem, you checked on Valerie and then made sure she got medical help immediately,' Colin reminded her. 'I was with you. You really couldn't have done any more than you did.'

'Once we'd identified the problem, I thought the hospital would be able to help her. I thought she might have to stay in for a couple of days while they got her back on her feet, but she'd recover and be able to go back to her flat. I just...' Georgina shook her head. 'I don't know what to say. What to do. I...' Her voice trailed off in misery.

'I know.' Colin squeezed her hand. 'Louise has shut the bakery and the mill until further notice, and Billy has closed the butchery as well. The food hygiene team is coming back to do a more detailed investigation into both of the businesses. Until their report comes back, there's nothing anyone can do.'

'Right now, I feel utterly helpless. And guilty – because the fact remains, if I hadn't taken Valerie that sausage roll, she'd still be alive now,' Georgina said. 'There has to be a way of finding out who's behind all this.'

Colin gave a dry cough. 'That *way* would be me and my team, doing our job. And yes, I know you and Sybbie have been amazing at untangling the truth behind the cold cases, but you really can't help us with this one, Georgie.'

She ignored the comment. 'You said Miss Hurst died from rat poison. Valerie Waring died from campylobacter. Isn't it a bit convenient that two deaths from two different causes are both linked to the same place, in the same week? It's almost as if some-one's trying to cover all the bases and make sure that something sticks.'

'It's an odd coincidence, I agree,' Colin said. 'And it needs investigating.' He sighed. 'The thing is, Louise and Billy have both worked with food for a long time, with no issues, and both of them are highly aware of food hygiene. They know the rules and they know what they're doing.' He ticked off the points on his fingers. 'Keeping raw and cooked foods separate, using different work surfaces and chopping boards for each, keeping raw meat in a sealed container in the bottom of the fridge so it can't drip onto other foods, washing hands thoroughly after handling raw food, and cleaning utensils thoroughly after use with raw food. They've done all the right things.' He shook his head. 'But *somehow* the bacteria still got into the chicken used for the sausage rolls.'

'Which might be accidental, though that seems dubious,' Georgina said. 'And *somehow* the rat poison got into Miss Hurst's sausage rolls – which certainly isn't likely to be accidental,' she added.

'You need solid evidence before you can make any accusations,' Colin said gently. 'If it was deliberate, how did the killer do it?

How would they even source the bacteria in the first place? Remember that campylobacter's a notifiable disease.'

'And there was the rat in the grain store,' Georgina continued. 'Louise checked with the pest controller – Riley the Rat Man – and he says he blocked up all the entry points. A rat couldn't have got in. Could someone – the person who interfered with the sausage rolls, perhaps – have deliberately put a dead rat into the grain store to make it look bad and point suspicion at Louise?'

'It's possible,' Colin said. 'You said Louise brought you flowers this afternoon. Did she talk to you about any of this?'

'Yes. Her husband's come back from London – he normally leaves Norfolk on Monday morning after breakfast and gets home for Friday teatime – so he can see a bit more of the kids. His mum's staying at the moment because there's a problem with her flat, but I get the impression she's more of a support to Louise than Hugo is,' Georgina said. 'I feel a bit sorry for Louise, actually. I think she moved here thinking it would be a lovely life for the kids and they'd be happier as a family here than they were in London, but it's turned out to be a nightmare. Apparently Hugo couldn't stand working from home and the commute's horrific, so he's working in London and living in this tiny little flat during the week. She's got the nanny to help her here, obviously, but she thinks the nanny's bored. What happens if the nanny gives her notice? How is she going to manage the kids and the business?'

'It can take a while to settle here when you've moved from London,' Colin said. 'You and I both know that. And I'm sure there are times when you've missed London, just as I do, every so often.'

'That's true,' Georgina agreed. 'But Louise loves it here and the kids are settled at school. Hugo is the only one of the family who doesn't like it here – well, and maybe the nanny. You know, even before everyone started being ill and her sausage rolls got the blame, I think Louise was struggling. Living apart from her husband for most of the week has obviously put a bit of a strain on her marriage, plus she's worried the nanny wants to leave. I think this new investigation might tip her over the edge.' Georgina sighed. 'Louise thinks everyone locally is going to see her as the modern equivalent of Typhoid Mary, someone who makes everyone else ill, and she's scared her business will go under. But nobody's made her an offer for the business; it isn't that someone's trying to drive her out so they can take over the mill.'

'That's an interesting theory,' Colin said. 'What made you think of that?'

'I didn't. It was, um, suggested to me,' Georgina said, feeling her face heat. Oh, no. Please don't let them have a fight about this now.

'Suggested by Doris?' Colin enquired mildly.

'Yes.' Georgina lifted her chin. 'And, actually, it was a good thought. If someone wanted the business and Louise had already refused to sell, they might've decided to put pressure on her another way, to make her want to leave and maybe sell the business at a lower price than the original offer. Plus there might be a link with Margaret Chorley's case. Except I haven't had a chance to look any further into that,' she admitted. 'My head's been all over the place.'

'You've had Bert to worry about,' Colin pointed out, 'and you're clearly worrying about Will, too.'

'I am.' Georgina sighed. 'This is shaping up to be a truly horrible week.'

He gave her a hug. 'I'm here for you. Always. And that goes for your kids, too. I'm not trying to take their dad's place or push myself in where I'm not wanted. I just want Will or Bea to know that if they need someone to talk to who isn't you – a sounding board, if you like – I'd be more than happy to help. And whatever they tell me will stay confidential. I might try and persuade them to talk to you, but I won't break any confidences.'

'That,' she said, 'is lovely of you. Thank you. I'll make sure they know. And I'd better break the news about Valerie to Sybbie and Jodie.'

· · ·

When Will walked into the kitchen, a couple of hours later, Bert wagged his tail but stayed put in his bed, clearly not feeling up to greeting the latest arrival with his usual exuberance.

Before Will could ask why Bert was so subdued, Colin smiled at him. 'Good to see you, Will. How was your journey?'

'Not so bad,' Will said, though he looked more serious than Georgina was used to and her heart lurched. What had rattled her son? Would he talk to her about it?

'Georgie, can I borrow your office while I make a couple of phone calls?' Colin asked.

'Sure.' She appreciated his tact, even though he was being a bit obvious in leaving mother and son alone together. 'Will, why don't you go and dump your stuff in your room while I put the kettle on? Coffee?'

'Decaf, please, if you have any,' Will said. 'Otherwise, camomile tea would be great.'

Which wasn't what she was used to from him at all. Will was a notorious caffeine fiend. Georgina kept a stock of camomile tea with honey and vanilla for Bea, so she made a mug of that for both of them, and took a mug of coffee through to Colin.

'He's not himself, is he?' Colin asked quietly.

'No. I just hope he'll talk to me,' Georgina said.

'Thanks, Mum,' Will said when he came downstairs.

'I was wondering, are you planning to stay just for the weekend, or a little longer?' she asked carefully.

'I don't really know. For a few days, if that's OK,' he said.

Again, that wasn't Will. He planned everything to the nth degree. The vagueness really worried her. 'Stay as long as you like. You know you always have a bed here.' She opened a tin of biscuits and placed it on the table, deciding to go for the direct approach. 'Want to talk about it?' she asked.

'No. And yes.' Will sighed. 'I'm old enough that I ought to be able to sort things out on my own.'

'True,' she said. 'But if you've got a problem, sometimes it helps to think out loud to someone else. You know I'm not going to judge you. Or if you don't want to talk to me, maybe you could talk to Colin. He's good at thinking things through and he won't break any confidences.' She coughed. 'I haven't broken any confidences, either, but he knows I worry about you. He said to tell you he wasn't trying to muscle in and take your dad's place, but he's there if you want to talk.'

'He's a good bloke, Colin,' Will said, and took a biscuit. 'And tell him thanks.'

He lapsed into a silence that lasted for so long that Georgina thought he wasn't going to open up to her, but then he sighed again. 'I've never taken sick leave before. But work's doing my head in.'

Sick leave? Now she was really worried. But she'd already pushed him; she didn't want to press any harder, in case it made him clam up. She waited, and after a couple of quiet sips of tea, he said, 'It's my new boss. Jill. I say "new", but she's been there six months now. She's a micromanager, and it drives us all up the wall.'

'Is it worth talking to HR about it?' Georgina suggested.

'Criticising their golden girl?' he asked, giving a bitter laugh. 'No. And HR aren't there for the staff, anyway. They're there for the company. All they're concerned about is covering their backs.' He grimaced. 'I can't stand the woman. And it's nothing to do with her being a woman, either, though I know you wouldn't think I've got that sort of view. It's her management style that gets to me – or, rather, lack of it. She wants updates all the time, and it's such a waste of resources. We spend more time writing reports for her than we spend actually doing our work. She's obsessed with the most minor details.' He narrowed his eyes in obvious disgust. 'I've never met such a nitpicker or a control freak. She explains everything to us as if we're a bunch of two-year-olds instead of us all having a doctorate, and it drives us all crazy. We've all looked up stuff on the internet about how to deal with micromanagers, and we've tried putting it into practice – but absolutely nothing seems to work with her. She's a nightmare.'

'Everyone else in your team has a problem with her, too?' Georgina asked.

Will nodded. 'Though she does seem to single me out in particular. I don't know whether she's got someone in mind for my job, but it feels as if she's looking for a way she can get rid of me. It's as if she thinks that if she keeps criticising me and questioning what I do all the time, and puts enough pressure on me, eventually I'll snap and she'll get the excuse she needs to sack me.'

'She can't do that,' Georgina said, outrage welling up. Who did this woman think she was?

'Try stopping her,' Will said. 'Two of my friends have already left. She used the same tactics on them, and brought in their replacements. Hand-picked. Interestingly, she doesn't seem to micromanage the new people.' He grimaced. 'So I'm very careful what I say in the office or the lab now.' Will worked for the government and whatever he actually did in the office or lab was covered by the Official Secrets Act, so Georgina knew not to ask him for details. 'I know it sounds as if I'm completely paranoid, but because she treats them differently, it makes me wonder if they're listening to everyone's conversations and then reporting everything back to her. The team definitely doesn't socialise as much together as we used to since she's been around. I can't remember the last time we went out for Friday night drinks, or for a pizza on payday.'

'Splitting the team? That sounds like classic divide and rule on her part,' Georgina said.

'The worst thing is, it's working. I feel uptight the whole time, Mum,' Will admitted. 'I lie awake half the night, dreading the idea of going to work in the morning. It's as much as I can do to drag myself out of bed and have a shower. It got to the point this week when I was actually wondering whether I could get away with putting poison in her coffee.'

Georgina knew he wouldn't actually do anything like that. Her son was a decent man. Though with the deaths and sickness caused by the poisoner at Great Wenborough Mill, and Margaret Chorley's case, his throwaway comment was a little too close for comfort. She reached over and squeezed his hand. 'I take it you've already tried all the sleep hygiene stuff?'

'Having a bath before bed, staying off my phone and my laptop in the evening, making sure the room's dark enough and cool enough – yeah.' Will grimaced. 'None of it worked. Or the stuff you spray on your pillow. I went to see my GP and asked for some sleeping tablets. She didn't give me any, but she asked a few more questions and she's signed me off for a week with stress.' He shrugged. 'Maybe she's right and it'll help a lot just not being in that bloody place for a few days. I feel bad that it's put extra pressure on the rest of the team, because they'll have my work to do as well as their own, but right now I think it's a choice between letting them down or ending up on a murder charge.'

'Oh, Will.' She gave him a hug. 'I'm so sorry you're having to deal with this sort of behaviour.' None of her friends or their children worked in HR, so she couldn't ask any of them for advice on how Will could change his boss's behaviour. 'But I hope you know you have my full backing. And I'll support you with anything I can – whether it's helping you put together a case so you can complain effectively to HR and make them get her to change her behaviour, or proofreading job applications.'

'I thought about just resigning. I've got enough savings to keep me going for a few months, until I find another job,' he said. 'But then that's giving in to her bullying, and it makes me look as if I'm not at all resilient or reliable – that I'll give up at the first hurdle I come to. Employers don't like that, so it's hardly going to help me find a new job.' He scowled. 'Plus I don't want her to win. She's the sort who'd do it by fair means or foul. Dad would have something to say about that.'

'For nothing can seem foul to those that win,' Georgina quoted. At Will's raised eyebrow, she said, '*Henry IV, Part One* – spoken by the king after the battle of Shrewsbury.'

'That's it exactly,' Will said.

'I can understand you not wanting to let her win,' Georgina said. 'But is staying there really worth the stress she's causing you?

You know you can always come here for as long as you need to. If you do need some money to tide you over, I can help with that, too.'

'I know, Mum, and I appreciate that.' He sighed. 'I just want to do the job I love without all this relentless and *pointless* interference. Is that so much to ask?'

'Of course it isn't.'

He blew out a breath. 'I think I need a bit of time to chill. Maybe I can take Bert for a w—' He broke off and gave his mother a rueful smile. 'I'd better not say that word in full and get him overexcited before dinner, had I?'

'And it'd only be a very short one, right now,' Georgina said. 'If you need a long one or a run, you might be better off borrowing Max and Jet from Sybbie.'

Will frowned. 'Why? What's happened?'

She told him about the sausage rolls, Bert's illness and Valerie's death.

'Oh, Mum.' He gave her a hug. 'I'm so sorry your friend died. And Bert's been so ill. I've been banging on about all the rubbish at work while you've been having just as much of a horrible time. Why didn't you tell me?'

'Hey. You weren't banging on, and besides, your problem's been going on for longer than mine,' she reminded him. 'I wish you'd said something to me earlier about how hard it's been for you.'

'It started the first week she was there. I kind of hoped it'd stop once she'd settled in,' Will said. 'But it's just got worse, day by day.' He frowned. 'How is it that nice people like Valerie get bumped off, and vile people like Jill just seem to sail through life, totally untouchable?'

'I don't know,' Georgina said. 'I guess poetic justice doesn't happen in real life.'

Will made a fuss of Bert. 'I thought he was a bit quiet when I came in, but then I thought I'm probably not seeing things as they really are because I'm so wound up about work. Now I know Bert's been so poorly, I understand why he wasn't bouncing around the way he usually does when I come home. The springy English springer.'

'More like a clinger spaniel, right now. That reminds me – you need to be really on point with your hand hygiene,' Georgina said. 'Bert's going to be infectious with the campylobacter for a few more days.'

'A zoonotic infection. That almost makes me want to bottle up all his doggy drool, take it back to Salisbury and dump it in Jill's cappuccino,' Will said, sounding very pleased with the idea.

'I'm going to pretend I didn't hear that,' Georgina said, narrowing her eyes at him. 'That isn't you, Will.'

He flushed, looking faintly guilty. 'Sorry. I know.'

'Though, if you're going to be home for a few days, I might pick your brains,' she said. Maybe giving him something to think about other than his problems at work might help to lower his stress. 'What do you know about arsenic?'

'Arsenic?' He looked surprised. 'Why? Are you working on an article about Napoleon's wallpaper or something like that?'

She explained about Margaret Chorley and the accusation of the poisoned flour leading to her trial and conviction. 'Apparently the poison used was arsenic.'

'Arsenic. Hmm. When did it happen?' Will asked.

'1845.'

'That makes sense. The Arsenic Act, regulating how arsenic was sold, didn't come in until 1851,' he said. 'And even then people could still get round it. Some of the pharmacists were a bit slack with their paperwork.'

'Will, should I be worried that you know about the history of arsenic sales in detail?' Georgina asked, thinking of his comment about wanting to poison his boss.

That got a laugh out of him. 'No. I did a project in my second year as an undergraduate on the uses of arsenic in the nineteenth century,' Will said. 'It was used in dyes because it made the colours stable and vibrant, and it was cheap so it was useful for mass-produced goods. Two of the most-used colours were Scheele's green and canary yellow, and arsenic was used in the production of both; it was in wallpaper, fabrics and paint.'

'Napoleon's wallpaper?' Georgina asked.

'Not just his,' Will said. 'A German chemist wrote in a news-paper that damp rooms with green wallpaper often smelled like mice, which he believed was caused by dimethyl arsenic acid within the wallpaper leaching out into the air. The thing is, arsenic poisoning would make people have headaches, nausea and fatigue; but anyone who complained of those symptoms back then would be shut up in a darkened room with the windows and doors closed to keep them warm and prevent chills.'

'Meaning they'd breathe in more of the arsenic from the wall-paper instead of the fresh air they needed, and it would make them even more ill,' Georgina said.

'Exactly,' Will said.

'And then there's Charlotte Perkins Gilman's novella, "The Yellow Wallpaper",' Georgina said. Literature was more her bag than chemistry. 'The narrator's illness is linked to the way she felt oppressed by society – but some of her symptoms sound like those of arsenic poisoning, and her wallpaper was yellow.'

'Arsenic was probably in her face powder, too,' Will said. 'You wouldn't believe how many things contained arsenic in Victorian times. Artificial flowers, stuffed animals, and even candles. And it was really easy to buy arsenic trioxide from a grocer's or chemist's shop. Before the Arsenic Act, some sellers would make a note of your name and insist on having a witness, but a lot of them just didn't bother. The Act changed that; from then on, the seller was supposed to record all sales in a special poison register, stating the date of sale, how much was sold, the name, address and occupation of the buyer, and why it was being bought. The seller and the buyer both had to sign the register; if the buyer couldn't write, the seller had to put "cannot write" in the space for the buyer's signa-ture. And pharmacists or grocers could only sell arsenic for non-medicinal purposes if they'd mixed it with soot or indigo first.'

'Indigo? People used to use indigo for laundry,' Georgina said.

'White fabric goes yellow when it fades, so adding a tiny bit of blue to the wash made it look white again. And surely that's poisonous in itself?'

Will nodded. 'But adding the colour to the arsenic meant there couldn't be any accidental poisoning, because the potential victims would see straight away that the food or drink had been adulterated with something.'

'A bowl of sugar or something light-coloured, maybe. But what if it was added to a rich, dark fruit cake?' Georgina asked. 'You wouldn't notice the colour. You wouldn't notice the taste, either, especially if the fruit had been soaked in alcohol or someone had poured alcohol into the cake regularly while it matured.'

'True,' Will said. 'A lethal dose of arsenic would be about two hundred milligrams. It's about the same density as flour.'

'And a level teaspoon of flour weighs about two and a half grams, if it's packed loosely. So we're talking about a tenth of a teaspoon of arsenic,' Georgina calculated, excitement quickening her pulse as she started to figure out what might have happened in Margaret's case. 'That's not very much at all.'

'It'd be easily hidden in a cup of tea – or, rather, in the sugar put in the tea,' Will agreed. 'Though, to be fair, most poisonings were accidental.'

'Colin said that poison was seen as a woman's weapon in those days,' Georgina mused.

'It was, though the stats were exaggerated by people who had an agenda. There were some suggested amendments to the Act that only men should be allowed to buy arsenic, though other people protested and it didn't get into the final bill,' Will said. 'Between the 1810s and the 1830s, the number of criminal trials for poisoning trebled, and in the next decade they went up by another fifty per cent. Mind you, after the Arsenic Act, although cases of arsenic poisoning decreased, there were even more cases of murder using other poisons.'

'I had no idea,' Georgina said.

'There were some fairly famous cases about murder using

arsenic in Victorian times,' Will said. 'There was a big one in Glasgow, in the 1850s. Madeleine Smith was from a rich family who wanted to marry her off to a suitable husband – except she'd been having a secret affair with a clerk and had promised to marry him. She asked him to return her letters, but he threatened to let everyone see them so she'd be forced to marry him.'

'But that's extortion. Surely that was illegal?' Georgina interrupted.

'You'd think. Then, a couple of weeks later, he was found dead from arsenic poisoning, and she was arrested for murder. She'd actually bought arsenic in the weeks leading up to his death, but the two chemists who sold it to her testified that they'd coloured their arsenic, and the prosecution said that the arsenic that killed her lover *hadn't* been coloured. The evidence was circumstantial and the jury said it was "not proven", so she got off,' Will finished. 'Even though most people thought she was guilty and there was a real scandal about it.'

'So it was possible for someone not to be found guilty, even if arsenic really was involved?' Georgina asked.

Will nodded. 'There was another case in Bradford, a year later, where a confectioner accidentally used arsenic trioxide instead of powdered gypsum in the sweets he sold on the market. Twenty people died and two hundred more were made ill, including the confectioner himself. The arsenic seller, his assistant and the confectioner were all arrested, but the judge said it was an accident and none of them were hanged for murder.'

She narrowed her eyes at him. 'I get that this is all from your undergraduate days, and it sounds as if you were fascinated with it at the time, but please tell me you haven't been considering using arsenic on your boss.'

'Oh, I have, but not *that* seriously.' He gave her a wry smile. 'It's not exactly easy to get hold of arsenic nowadays. There was a late Victorian case where the alleged poisoner, Florence Maybrick, apparently extracted arsenic from flypapers by soaking them in water. But for decades now arsenic has been phased out as an ingredient in pesticides and wood preservatives, mainly because people started realising the environmental effects on groundwater and the like. It's still used in lead and copper specialist alloys, the manufacturing of semiconductors, and some glass and ceramics,' he added. 'But, no. I'm not going to put arsenic in Jill's coffee.'

'Good,' she said. 'And on that note, I'll switch on the electric steamer for the veg, and heat the jambalaya through for dinner.' She smiled at him. 'I hope it's still your favourite.'

'It is. I love your jambalaya,' Will said. 'Thanks, Mum.' He gave her a hug. 'I already feel a bit better. Just being here, miles away from work, and talking to you about interesting stuff, makes me feel more – well, *normal*.'

Even though discussions about arsenic and murder definitely weren't part of normal family life, Georgina thought. 'I'm glad,' she said. 'And if you want to distract yourself a bit while you're here, you could always help Sybbie and me sift through the evidence about Margaret Chorley.'

'Count me in. I'd love to help,' Will said with a smile.

NINE

They spent the evening quietly after dinner, and Will excused himself to have a long bath and an early night. Georgina messaged Sybbie to let her know that Bert was doing OK, and Will was home and would help them work on Margaret's case. Sybbie replied that she'd be over in the morning, as Bernard was off to an exhibition of maps, but she'd leave Max and Jet with Giles and Cesca.

Georgina and Colin sat on the sofa with Bert wedged happily between them, snoozing.

'It's good to have Bert back home,' Colin said.

'Definitely.' She stroked the spaniel's soft fur.

Colin lowered his voice. 'Did Will open up to you?'

She nodded. 'I told him what you said. He appreciates the offer and he might take you up on it.' She blew out a breath. 'I think he needs some time away from work, though. Let's just say the world could do with more Valeries and fewer people like his boss.'

'Got you,' Colin said. 'If he talks to me, I'll act as if I know nothing. But it's tricky when you have to work with someone you don't get on with, especially if they can pull rank and make your life difficult. The only way to get through it is to cover yourself and double-check everything you do – and that's a real strain.'

'That sounds like experience talking,' she said, trying to keep her tone light.

'Not mine,' he said. 'I've been very lucky. My boss supported me when anyone else would have made sure I was kicked out of the Force. But, yes, I've known people who struggled, usually when a new boss tries to make themselves look important. It settles down after a while.'

'I think that's what Will hoped the situation would be here, but it's already been quite a while and she's still difficult,' she said with a sigh. 'Hopefully being here for a few days will give him a different perspective, or at least help him make a decision about how to handle it. He's going to help Sybbie and me sift through the papers for Margaret Chorley's case, and that will hopefully distract him and stop him worrying about his work situation.'

'Usually Bea's the one who helps you with the cold cases,' Colin said.

'I know. But this involves arsenic, and, with Will's knowledge of chemistry, he can probably tell us more than Bea could,' Georgina reminded him.

Bert was definitely brighter the next morning. Colin left to meet Larissa so they could interview Billy and Louise. Georgina and Will had both set up their laptops at the kitchen table, and Georgina had shown him the material she'd found so far about Margaret, including the broadside with its hideous woodcut.

Sybbie arrived with lemon cake from Francesca, a fuss for Bert, a hug for Will, and a cheery, 'Marvellous to see you, dear boy! How are you?'

'I'm fine,' Will said, smiling back, though Georgina knew that he wasn't telling the truth.

'Your mum tells me you're going to help us with Margaret Chorley's case. Excellent,' Sybbie said. 'I spent yesterday going through a bit more of Amelia's diary, and I've photographed the relevant bits and put the photos on my laptop, so I can blow it up to a more readable size. I brought the diary with me as well.'

'Amelia being Bernard's ancestor?' Will queried.

'His great-great-great-grandmother,' Sybbie said. 'Obviously she lived in Little Wenborough, whereas Margaret's family lived in the mill at Great Wenborough, but the two villages are close enough for everyone to know what was going on in the other village as well as their own. I take it your mum's brought you up to speed on what we've found so far?'

'She has,' Will confirmed.

Sybbie set up her laptop next to Will's and Georgina's, and Will pored over the photographs of Amelia's diary while Georgina made coffee.

'It's good to see this one looking a bit more like his usual happy self,' Sybbie said, stroking the top of Bert's head. He gave a tiny wag of his tail and rested his chin on her knee.

'Doris sat with him on Thursday night,' Georgina said. 'Which made me feel a lot better, because it meant he wasn't alone.'

'Is Doris going to be joining us today?' Will asked.

'I hope so,' Georgina said.

'But you don't actually know?'

Georgina shook her head.

'So how does it work? Do you have some kind of signal to contact Doris?' Will asked.

'No. I have to wait until she starts talking to me – though she does keep in touch quite frequently,' Georgina said. 'Since being reunited with Harrison, she's not around quite as much as she used to be. Which in a way I'm glad about, because they're together again now.'

'But she's your friend and you miss chatting to her about Shakespeare,' Will said.

'I'm afraid I'm not quite on a par with Doris when it comes to Shakespeare,' Sybbie said. 'I have to look things up!'

'Ah, but you and I have other things in common.' Georgina

gave a hammy wink. 'A certain gallery in Holt. And the antique shops I'm meant to steer you out of.'

'You can *try*, dear girl.' Sybbie gave a deliberate, cackling laugh.

'Obviously I can hear Doris through my hearing aids, but nobody else can,' Georgina said, turning back to Will. 'She can hear any questions you ask, but I'll need to repeat her answers for you.' She gave him a rueful smile. 'I know it sounds weird, and ridiculous, and utterly unlikely, but...'

'There are more things in heaven and earth, Horatio,' Sybbie said. 'Which is what your Stephen would have quoted, too.'

'Wouldn't he just?' Will chuckled. 'Dad loved *Hamlet*.' He turned to Georgina. 'And Colin believes you now about Doris, Mum?'

'He's getting there,' Georgina said. 'I think it helped that you, as a sensible scientist, didn't dismiss her existence out of hand. And sometimes Bert wags his tail as if he's greeting a friend, when there's nobody there. Colin's witnessed that a couple of times now, and I think he accepts that Bert can see things he can't.'

'I know it was a bit tricky between you last year, but I'm glad you didn't split up over it,' Will said. 'I think he's good for you – and you're good for him.'

Georgina smiled at her son. 'Yes. You're right.' She brought the coffee over to the table. 'So what does Amelia's journal say, Sybbie?'

'You remember that in April, she wrote that Herbert Forrest's little boy had died, poisoned by a cake,' Sybbie said. 'A couple of weeks later, she wrote that Forrest had accused Margaret Chorley of sending the poisoned flour used to make the cake, and she was quite shocked because she didn't think it likely. Margaret's father was the miller in Great Wenborough, and Margaret had been running the mill very efficiently during the previous year, since her father became unwell. The manor used Chorley's Mill to grind the corn from their estate.'

'Alfred Chorley. I found his name in the trade directories,'

Georgina said. 'And how interesting that Bernard's family used the mill in the next village rather than the one here.'

'I take it Herbert Forrest owned the mill in Little Wenborough, then?' Sybbie asked.

'Yes. Actually, the trade directories list him as a mill-owner in several of the villages around here, and also as a corn factor.'

'Like the Mayor of Casterbridge,' Sybbie said immediately. 'Maybe Forrest was as difficult as Henchard.'

'Ah, but did Forrest try to sell his wife?' Will asked.

Sybbie smiled in appreciation of the fact he'd picked up her reference to Michael Henchard selling his wife in Hardy's novel. 'Not as far as we know, but I rather get the impression from Amelia that he was the type who would have happily sold his own grand-mother,' she said.

'Doris said something about Forrest having a "golden thumb" – being a cheat, basically,' Georgina said thoughtfully. 'I thought it might be worth looking through the newspaper archives to see if there had been any accusations in the press. There might be someone with a grudge against him. I have an account with one of the genealogy sites, and it has a section of digitised local newspa-pers; best of all, they're searchable, so we're not going to have to look through every issue.'

'What we're looking for are any references to Herbert Forrest and any references to Margaret Chorley, between April 1845 when she was accused of the murder and August 1845 when she was hanged,' Will checked.

'Let's go back a couple of years,' Georgina said, 'in case we find something about Forrest being accused of cheating. And we need to look up Margaret's dad, too.'

'We're looking for three different people. Let's take one each. Will, who do you want to research?' Sybbie asked.

'Forrest,' Will said.

'I'll do Alfred, and you do Margaret, Georgie?' Sybbie suggested.

Between them, they got to work on the searches.

'I've got a newspaper ad,' Will said, a couple of minutes later. 'From 1842. Listen to this. "A malicious and unfounded report has lately been circulated, injurious to the character of Mr Herbert Forrest of Great Wenborough in the County of Norfolk, Miller, stating that he has adulterated his flour and been fined by the Magistrates for doing so. He has not been found guilty of the alleged behaviour and declares the report is false. He will prosecute any person or persons with the utmost rigor of the law, who may vilify his character."'

'It sounds as if people have been talking about him. And he wasn't found guilty, so does that mean he was actually brought up before the bench for cheating?' Sybbie asked. 'He lived in Little Wenborough, so Bernard's great-great-great-grandfather, William, would have been the magistrate.'

'Meaning it's highly unlikely that Forrest paid off the magistrate,' Will said. 'Assuming that William was the same kind of person as Bernard.'

'Scrupulously honest? Yes,' Sybbie said. 'Everything we found out about the family when we were researching Timothy Marsden's case says Bernard's family were good people. Though I'm afraid we can't say the same of the people who lived at Great Wenborough Hall. What if, somehow, Forrest managed to get his case tried there, or in another village where he owned a mill, and perhaps had the local magistrate in his pocket?'

'I looked back through the editions before the ad, and there's a report in the *Norfolk Chronicle* a couple of months earlier,' Will said. 'Lord Rutherford, the magistrate at Great Wenborough, was due to hear a case against Herbert Forrest for adulteration of flour, but the plaintiff dropped the complaint and said it was a mistake.'

'Was it really a mistake?' Georgina asked. 'It's not too much of a stretch to wonder whether whoever made the complaint was pressured into dropping the case — either by Forrest or by Rutherford.'

'Given what we know about the Rutherford family in the past, it could be either,' Sybbie said. 'I've come up with next to nothing on Alfred Chorley, other than a mention of his name in reports about Margaret.'

'Forrest tried to pressure Alfred into selling Great Wenborough Mill to him, for a ridiculously low price,' Doris said. 'Margaret persuaded her dad not to sell to him, and she went to the local magistrate to complain. But Rutherford refused to do anything about it. He said Forrest had done nothing wrong, offering to buy the mill.'

Georgina repeated the comment to the others.

'Doris is here now? Hello, Doris,' Will said. 'I haven't "met" you properly yet, but I assume you know I'm Will, Georgina's son.'

'She knows,' Georgina said with a smile. 'She saw you at the Regency Theatre when we all went to support Bea last.'

'I'm pleased to meet you, Doris,' Will said. 'Any friend of my mum's is a friend of mine.'

'She's pleased to meet you, too,' Georgina reported.

'Before we go any further, Georgie, I have a message for you from Valerie,' Doris said. 'You're not to blame yourself for what happened to her. She says it wasn't your fault. You weren't to know that someone had tampered with the sausage rolls. And it's not your fault that Bert's been ill, either. Spaniels are horribly greedy, and she knows you love him as much as she did and you look after him well.'

There was a huge lump in Georgina's throat, and she had to blink back tears. 'Thank you,' she whispered. She pulled herself together. Just. 'Anyway. We were talking about Alfred Chorley. Margaret told Doris earlier that her dad's mind was starting to wander a bit.'

'Which sounds a bit like the early stages of dementia, and that would have made him vulnerable,' Will said. 'The more I'm learning about this Herbert Forrest guy, the more shady I think he is. And the magistrate really said it was OK for Forrest to offer Alfred Chorley a pittance for his mill?' He shook his head. 'Unbelievable.'

'It's worse than that,' Doris said grimly. 'When Margaret

pointed out he'd offered well under what it was worth, Rutherford just said that women didn't have a head for business.'

Georgina repeated the comment to the others.

'What? That's *outrageous*,' Sybbie said, pursing her lips. 'Who did Rutherford think ran the big houses? It certainly wasn't the lord of the manor! I'm very glad Bernard's family didn't take such a ridiculously outmoded view.' She shook her head. 'But why on earth didn't Margaret talk to William Walters? He was a magistrate, for pity's sake, and he was a good man. I'm sure he would have helped her deal with Forrest.'

'Maybe she had to go to Rutherford, if he was the magistrate for Great Wenborough and that's where her mill was,' Will said.

'But Forrest lived in Little Wenborough, so there was a connection here, too,' Georgina said. 'I wonder how many of the other mills in Forrest's empire were sold to him at well below the market price?'

'And nobody would complain because he had the local magistrate on his side,' Sybbie said. 'I wouldn't be surprised if he gave Rutherford special rates for milling, to keep him sweet.'

'It sounds as if Forrest had a grudge against Margaret, because she wouldn't let her dad practically give the windmill to him,' Will said. 'And that's maybe why he thought up the scheme to accuse her of poisoning the flour. If he could get her thrown into jail, there wouldn't be anyone to help Alfred stand up to him – and then he could buy the mill as cheaply as he wanted.'

'He might have had the ear of the local magistrate,' Georgina said, 'but he wouldn't have had the same opportunity to corrupt the Assize judges. Why didn't they see that the case against Margaret was a put-up job?'

'Let's look at the evidence,' Will said. 'Did you find the trial reports in the papers, Mum?'

'I did,' Georgina said, and they all crowded round her laptop so they could see them. 'Before the trial itself, there was the inquest into the little boy's death. Their expert witness tested the contents of his stomach and found arsenic. Obviously Catherine Forrest was devastated by the death of her only child; according to the papers, she was an invalid, and the distress made her illness even worse. And then Herbert Forrest claimed that Margaret Chorley was the one who'd sent them the poisoned flour.'

'Where was the proof?' Will asked.

'At the trial, a grocer from Bawburgh, a village just down the road, testified that he'd sold Margaret some arsenic to keep the mill clear of rats,' Georgina said. 'Though he didn't write down her name or the quantity of arsenic she bought, so he didn't have proof of what he actually sold her. It was just his word against hers. He said she bought it from him; she said she didn't.'

'It was before the Arsenic Act, so he didn't have to keep a register of purchases – and he didn't have to dye the poison with soot or indigo, either,' Will reminded her. 'But you're right. Without proof of whether he sold arsenic to her or not, how would the judge or jury know who to believe? And why would they believe him over her?' He frowned. 'Were all jurors male, back then?'

'I'll check,' Georgina said. She typed a quick question into the search engine on her laptop. 'Yes. Under the Juries Act 1825, a juror had to be male, aged between twenty-one and sixty, and they had to either own or lease a certain amount of land, or pay the poor rate on a property with at least fifteen windows.' She read on further. 'Juries were all-male until 1919. The only exception was a jury of matrons – if a woman was found guilty of a crime and sentenced to death, but she said she was pregnant, a jury of women were brought in to decide whether she was pregnant. If she was pregnant, then the death sentence tended to be commuted, or at the very least delayed until after the baby was born.'

'Maybe I'm showing bias, here, but I think an all-male jury would be more likely to take a male witness's word over Margaret's,' Sybbie said. 'They'd believe the grocer simply because he was one of them and she wasn't.'

'Margaret says she didn't buy anything from that grocer. She always went to the chemist in Great Wenborough when she wanted to buy arsenic to deal with the rats,' Doris said.

'Surely that would be easy to prove?' Will asked when Georgina relayed the information. 'Why didn't the lawyer ask the chemist she usually went to? Even if they hadn't written anything down, they would have been able to tell the jury that Margaret was a regular customer, and roughly how often she bought arsenic and how much she usually asked for. They'd know if she bought extra on any occasion, but they'd also know if she did nothing out of the ordinary.'

'It doesn't make sense that Margaret would make a special trip to another village and a different supplier, when she already had a stock of arsenic at the mill and a regular supplier in her own village,' Georgina agreed. 'Why wasn't that questioned at the trial?'

'Admitting to buying arsenic at all was probably enough to make them think she was guilty, even though using it to keep the rats under control in the mill was a very valid reason,' Sybbie said. 'I have more questions, too. Surely anyone eating the cake would have been able to taste there was something wrong from the very first bite? And wouldn't they have started being ill fairly quickly after eating it?'

'Arsenic trioxide – that's the form sold to customers – doesn't taste of anything,' Will said. 'It was cheap and easy to buy, you could dissolve it easily in water, and it looked like baking powder or powdered sugar so you could add it to food or drink without anyone being suspicious. Well, obviously until after they'd consumed it, started being ill, and died.'

'How quickly would people become ill?' Georgina asked.

'Within a few hours, I believe,' Will said. 'The symptoms of arsenic poisoning are really similar to those of cholera or gastroenteritis – nausea, stomach pain, and watery diarrhoea. I remember reading that a lot of arsenic poisoning cases went undetected in the early 1800s because the deaths were blamed on cholera or food poisoning, though that's impossible to prove, of course.'

'The evidence is all circumstantial,' Georgina said. 'Margaret had access to arsenic and obviously as a miller she had easy access to flour. But that doesn't mean she actually put the arsenic in the flour that the housekeeper used to make the cake. She might've mixed the arsenic with something sweet to use as bait for the rats in the mill, and someone took some of it when she was grinding corn and was too busy to notice them taking it.'

'For rodents, people often mixed the arsenic with flour and honey, making it into a paste,' Will said. 'When I did that uni research project I told you about, Mum, there was a case reported in one of the medical journals about a toddler whose mum had left a cupboard door open in the kitchen. She left the room for a minute, and came back to find him eating paste out of a box – and it was the mixture she'd made up for dealing with mice. Even though she gave him something straightaway to make him sick, it was already too late; he died later that day.'

'Oh, no. That's so sad,' Georgina said. 'The poor woman would never have forgiven herself for taking her eyes off him.'

'Amelia wrote more about Margaret's case in her diary around the time of the trial,' Sybbie said. 'She said Margaret's father was poorly and the girl had worked really hard to keep the mill going. She didn't think Margaret would have had the time to think about poisoning the flour, let alone take the package over to Forrest's house from Chorley's Mill. Besides, Forrest owned all those other mills. Who's to say that the flour and the arsenic didn't come from one of them rather than Chorley's Mill?'

'There was definitely arsenic in the cake,' Will said. 'It says here they used the Marsh test to test the little boy's stomach contents.'

'The Marsh test?' Georgina asked.

'It was pretty much the first big test in forensic toxicology,' Will explained. 'Marsh was called as an expert witness in a case in the 1830s where John Bodle was accused of poisoning his grandfather's coffee, and the jury wasn't convinced of Bodle's guilt because the forensic evidence didn't stand up. The problem was, Marsh had had to use Hahnemann's test, where you added hydrogen sulphide gas to an acidic solution. If arsenic was present, the chemical reaction would make arsenic trisulphide, which shows up as a bright yellow solid. But if you were testing the contents of someone's stomach, sometimes it affected the test and masked the results. Plus the test results tended to degrade pretty quickly, so the test had limited use as forensic evidence,' he continued. 'Bodle was found innocent, even though he later confessed to having poisoned his grandfather. Marsh decided to invent a better test for arsenic that would stand up in court. The Marsh test mixes the sample in a glass tube with hydrochloric acid and zinc, which produces a gas. When the gas is heated in a glass tube, any arsenic shows up on the glass as a silver-black metallic glaze.'

'I'm not sure if I should even ask how you know this stuff,' Sybbie said with a shudder.

'An undergraduate project on forensic tests and arsenic – I told Mum about it yesterday,' Will said with a smile. 'The Marsh test was famously used in a trial in France in 1840, when Marie Lafarge was accused of poisoning her husband with arsenic in cakes. Ironically, the prosecution messed up the test and the results were negative – but then the defence's expert witness did the test properly and proved that her late husband's stomach contents really did contain arsenic.'

'Hang on – the *defence's* witness was the one who proved Lafarge was guilty of feeding her husband arsenic?' Sybbie asked.

Will nodded. 'It was the big, shocking twist in the case. She was found guilty, and from then on the Marsh test was used for forensic evidence in arsenic poison trials.'

'Is it still used today?' Doris asked, and Georgina put the question to Will.

Will shook his head. 'You'd use molecular-absorption spectrophotometry. But it really made a difference back in its day.'

'According to the newspaper reports, the lawyer did a very showy performance during the trial – flinging flour from the bag into the fireplace, which made the room smell of garlic,' Georgina said. 'That convinced the jury that the arsenic was in the flour.'

'It's not the arsenic itself that smells of garlic,' Will said. 'It's the gas produced when arsenic is heated – arsine. As you say, Mum, it's showmanship, but it isn't a reliable test and the judges would have known that. Which is probably why they asked a pharmacist to do the Marsh test on the stomach contents of Forrest's son.'

'I've been making notes,' Doris said. 'I'll talk to Margaret again and see if any of this jogs her memory.'

'Good idea,' Georgina said, and told the others what Doris had suggested.

'Amelia's diary doesn't mention anything about the testing,' Sybbie said thoughtfully. 'Though she does say that William refused to use Forrest's Mill to grind the corn from their estate, even though Forrest's was nearer than Chorley's, because Forrest tended to give people back much less than they brought in to be milled.'

'Maybe that's where the adulteration claim came in,' Will said. 'If Forrest had been caught giving short measures, then maybe he added chalk or what have you to the flour, to increase the weight.'

'Sharp practice,' Georgina agreed.

'Amelia said Chorley's Mill was much more reliable,' Sybbie continued. 'She said William believed Forrest had either bribed or threatened people to lie in court for him.'

'And the prosecution came up with a convincing motive for Margaret to poison the flour,' Georgina said. 'Four different people swore on oath that they saw Margaret canoodling with Forrest. They claimed they'd heard her say she would get rid of Forrest's wife so he could marry her, and they more or less claimed the poisoned flour was aimed at Catherine Forrest.' She sighed. 'Except we know that's not true. Margaret refused to sleep with Forrest – which is another grudge he had against her – and she definitely didn't want to even kiss him, much less have sex with him or marry him.'

'Which means that the witnesses perjured themselves in court,' Will said. 'I think William Walters was right. Either Forrest bribed them or he threatened them. Maybe he employed them, and if they didn't do what he said, he would have sacked them and made sure they couldn't get another job.'

'Bully-boy tactics,' Sybbie said.

A bullying boss. Georgina's heart squeezed. This was meant to be taking Will's mind off his problems, not reflecting them. 'I wondered why the jury believed the poisoned flour was meant for Catherine Forrest, Herbert's wife. If Margaret had argued with Forrest, surely he would be the one she wanted to poison? But it says in the trial report that Catherine was an invalid who couldn't eat solid food. The housekeeper used to thicken milk with flour for her, and she'd drink that.'

'Milk thickened with flour?' Will looked up something on his laptop. 'Apparently it was known as "pap", and it was given to babies as well as invalids.'

'Flour and milk isn't exactly the best nutrition,' Sybbie said. 'I thought invalids were given beef tea and jellies that would be gentle on their stomach but would help to build up their strength?'

'That sounds more like something from Mrs Beeton, and her book didn't come out until the 1860s,' Georgina said.

'Oh, now this is *gross*,' Will said, continuing to scan his screen. 'An alternative to the flour-and-milk stuff was bread soaked in milk – and it says here that for babies, the nurse would chew it first.' He pulled a face. 'Poor Catherine. She would have known that, too, and thought about it while she choked down the food. Imagine if you're feeling ill to start with, and someone gives you this disgusting gloop mixed with someone else's saliva to drink, and you basically have to suck it through a spout at the side of a cup while you're lying down.' He wrinkled his nose. 'Though I suppose if she'd been given the arsenic-laced flour, at least she wouldn't have been able to taste the poison.'

'If the "thickened milk" was standard fare for invalids,' Georgina said, 'everyone in the village would have known that Catherine Forrest was an invalid and what she was being fed. But what I don't understand is why the housekeeper accepted an anonymous parcel of flour in the first place. Given that Forrest owned all those mills and was a corn dealer, surely the household had their own ready supply of flour?'

'That's a question I would have expected the defence to raise,' Will said.

'They didn't,' Georgina said. 'It simply seems to be an accepted fact that the flour arrived at his house.'

'Maybe it was seen as a kindness – Margaret, being a decent woman, sent the flour because she knew that's all that poor Catherine could manage to eat and wanted to help. Maybe she'd ground the flour in a special way, or something, to make it mix with the milk more easily,' Sybbie suggested. 'But everyone knows everyone else's business in a small village. The people in Great Wenborough would have known that Forrest was trying to cheat Albert Chorley out of his mill, and that there was no love lost between Forrest and Margaret. Surely someone would have wondered why she would send flour to the wife of a man she considered her enemy? Unless, of course, Catherine was actually her friend.'

'Margaret was framed,' Doris said.

Just as Louise Wilkins was being framed now, Georgina thought.

'It would be a nicely ironic way of putting an end to Forrest, though,' Will said. 'Just supposing Margaret *did* add the arsenic to the flour and sent it to Forrest's house. Given how greedy Forrest was, she might have guessed that he would order the housekeeper to use it for his benefit rather than his wife's.'

'So instead of making the pap for Catherine, the housekeeper made a cake for him – a cake that Catherine couldn't eat, the servants weren't allowed to touch, and the little boy shouldn't have touched. Except it was too tempting, and Daniel ate something that was intended for his father,' Georgina said.

'But Doris has already told us Margaret didn't send the flour. And we know that Forrest wasn't a nice man. I'd guess he didn't treat

Catherine particularly well. She might even have become an invalid as a way of avoiding him, because she wouldn't have been able to divorce him. What if,' Sybbie said, 'the housekeeper was really loyal to her mistress and hated the way Forrest treated Catherine? She could have claimed that the parcel of flour was sent to the house as a gift for Catherine, but really it was flour that was already in the larder. And maybe she added the arsenic to it herself, intending it for Forrest. After all, as the housekeeper, she would have been the one who ordered arsenic from the grocer's to deal with any vermin in the house. She had the motive, the means and the opportunity.'

'What about the other servants?' Georgina asked. 'Where did their loyalties lie – with Catherine or with Forrest?' She paused. 'Or there's another alternative, which is even nastier. Forrest was tired of having an invalid for a wife, so *he* was the one who spiked the flour with arsenic, intending to get rid of the wife he didn't want any more. Margaret was a convenient scapegoat because everyone in the two villages knew he'd tried to buy Chorley's Mill and she'd put a stop to it. If he claimed that she was the one who sent the poisoned flour to his house, people might believe she'd sent the poison to him.'

'I'm still a bit stuck on the "parcel of flour",' Sybbie said. 'Back then, dried goods would have been stored in bulk in the shops, and customers would have brought their own containers with them. People shopped locally, as and when they needed things. When were paper bags first used?'

Will looked it up. 'The 1850s. Maybe shopkeepers used greaseproof paper or brown paper and tied it with string to wrap up loose goods – say flour, sugar or rice – if a customer hadn't brought a tin with them?'

'That would make sense,' Sybbie said.

'The problem is,' Will said quietly, 'all this happened nearly two hundred years ago. Any evidence of who did what is long gone.'

'Or is it?' Doris asked. 'Margaret says she's looking for something. That's why she moves things around in the mill from time to time. She's not sure what, but she'll know it when she finds it.'

'Maybe if you tell her our different theories about who actually put the arsenic in the flour and why,' Georgina said, 'it might jog her memory. If we know what she's looking for, it might also help us to help Louise.'

'I'll do my best to prompt her,' Doris said.

TEN

'Forty-three years I've been a butcher,' Billy said, 'and my dad before me, and my grandad before him. My daughter Sheena's been working with me since she left school. She'll be taking over when I retire next year – I promised the wife I'd retire while we were still young enough to enjoy travelling and the like.' He indicated the younger woman sitting next to him, though even if he hadn't introduced her, Colin could see the family resemblance. 'Just over a hundred years, my family's had the shop. And we've never, ever had anything like this happen before.'

'We don't cut corners when we handle the raw meat and poultry or when we store it. The contamination didn't come from us,' Sheena said.

'All right, so our meat isn't as cheap as you'd buy from the supermarkets,' Billy said. 'But everyone knows they can trust us. Whatever you buy from us is fully traceable, with minimum food miles, and we know the animal welfare at our suppliers is top notch. We wouldn't accept anything less.'

'Campylobacter is actually in most poultry. But it grows really slowly, and it's killed if you cook the meat properly,' Sheena said. 'The problems happen when you don't – that's why it's known as the "barbecue bug". Food poisoning bacteria don't grow in the freezer or when meat's refrigerated below four degrees centigrade. But at a barbecue...' She shook her head. 'The meat's piled up on a plate outside on a nice sunny day. Even in the shade, it's at just the temperature where the bacteria will grow at its quickest. People handle the raw meat and the cooked meat without washing their hands in between, and they don't make sure the food's cooked right through – it smells good, so they think it'll be all right. And it isn't. How many times have you eaten a barbecued chicken drumstick and there's a bit of pink in the middle, next to the bone?'

Colin grimaced. 'Got you.' He paused. 'So you think the contamination must have happened at the bakery?'

'That's what bothers me,' Billy said. 'Louise knows her stuff, just as we do. Honestly, and I'm sorry to say it, I think someone must have tampered with her sausage rolls. But I have no idea who or why, and whether they're trying to ruin her business or ours.'

'And I hate to think that someone in our community would do this. It's not just the businesses, it's the villagers they're targeting,' Sheena added. 'Who in their right mind would want to poison a class of nine-year-olds and their teacher? And what happened to poor Valerie Waring – that's just terrible. She was always such a nice woman.'

'Georgie blames herself for that,' Colin said.

'She wasn't to know the sausage rolls were poisoned,' Billy said. 'And she loves that dog of hers like a child. No way would she put him in danger.'

'Bert's on the mend now,' Colin said. 'He's a bit subdued, but he's going to be all right.'

'At least that's one bit of good news,' Sheena said.

'You're absolutely sure you can't think of anyone you might have upset?' Colin asked.

'No,' Billy said. 'I mean, there's always some people you get on with better than others, but when you're in business you try to be pleasant to everyone. And of course the customers grumble about prices going up, but they know we try to absorb as much of the costs as we can and we're not profiteering.' He gave a wry chuckle.

'All you have to do is mention how much the electricity bill went up this month. Everyone's in the same boat.'

'If you think of anything, no matter how small,' Colin said, 'please get in touch. But right now we're stuck on leads.'

'The teacher was killed by rat poison, wasn't she?' Sheena asked.

'I can't really discuss that,' Colin said.

'Louise told me,' Sheena said. 'It's weird that the kids and some of the villagers were made sick by the campylobacter, but the teacher was killed by rat poison. Why would you use two different things to poison people or give them food poisoning? Unless someone was trying to hide the rat poison with the food poisoning – a sort of double bluff.' She shook her head. 'None of it really makes sense. The only thing I do know is that we need to clear our name, Inspector. We want to go back to serving our customers, and we want them to know it's safe to buy from us.'

'The council's food safety team will be round to see you,' Colin said, 'and they're the ones who can confirm you're a safe supplier. I'm sorry. I know it's frustrating for you – believe me, it's frustrating for me as well. I want to know who's behind this, and I want the community to be safe from whoever's behind the poisoning.'

'I really hope,' Billy said, 'that you don't think *we're* behind it.'

He didn't, but he couldn't really say that yet. 'I'll be in touch,' Colin said. 'And if you can think of anything relevant, no matter how obscure or daft it might seem, please let me know.'

Georgina, Sybbie and Will were taking a break from research and were discussing what had happened to Margaret Chorley. Georgina had made more coffee – she was relieved to see that Will was back to drinking coffee as normal – and opened a packet of chocolate biscuits, most of which had been scoffed by Will. Meanwhile Bert was curled in his basket, dozing and occasionally snoring.

'The rest of the newspaper reports are all quite gloomy,'

Georgina said. 'When Margaret was arrested, because she was going to be tried for murder at the Assizes, she was taken straight to the County Gaol and House of Correction.'

'In other words, the prison in Norwich Castle,' Sybbie said. 'I know they built a new prison there in the 1820s, but I think it was still pretty grim – dark, cold and damp.'

'Throughout the trial, Margaret protested her innocence, but the jury just didn't listen to her. Maybe it was because the murder victim was a child and the case made them think of their own children, so they were reacting with their emotions instead of looking at the facts. Maybe they didn't approve of a spinster running a business and thought they'd make an example of her, so she'd be a warning to other women who had ideas above their station. Or maybe, like the witnesses who claimed they heard her say she'd get rid of Forrest's wife, they'd been bribed or threatened by Forrest. They knew if they didn't find her guilty, he would exact his revenge on them later.' Georgina spread her hands. 'Whatever the reasons behind it, they found her guilty. She was sentenced to hang. The prison chaplain accompanied her to the scaffold, and the sentence was carried out.'

'And we know that prisoners who were executed were buried at the castle rather than in a churchyard, so her dad couldn't even bury her or visit her grave,' Sybbie added.

'It was a real miscarriage of justice,' Will said. 'What happened to Margaret's dad after her execution?'

'I'd have to look that up in the records,' Georgina said, 'but I'd guess that if he didn't have any other family to take him in, he probably ended up in the local workhouse infirmary and died there.'

'So Forrest did manage to get his hands on the mill?' Sybbie asked.

'With Margaret dead, there wouldn't have been anyone to stop him bullying Alfred Chorley into selling,' Georgina said. 'Put it this way, I took a look in the online trade directories, and Forrest's name is listed next to Little Wenborough Mill in 1848.'

'That doesn't sit well with me,' Will said, frowning. 'Forrest lied, Margaret was hanged because of his lies, and then he went on to steal her family's business and make a fat profit.'

'Sadly, dear boy, life isn't always fair,' Sybbie said with a sigh. 'But the one thing we can do now is to try to prove Margaret's innocence.'

'Without any proof?' Will asked.

'We'll just keep going through the records, and with any luck Doris will come back with more information from Margaret,' Georgina said. 'Let's divvy up the searches and give it another hour. Will, do you want to see what else comes up in the newspapers? Sybbie, could you go further in Amelia's diary? And I'll try the births, deaths and marriages, to see if I can trace what happened to Alfred and the Forrests.'

'Can I help you?' The fair-haired man who answered the door to Mill Cottage sounded perfectly pleasant, but his ice-blue eyes were narrowed in suspicion.

Which was understandable, Colin thought, given what had been happening around here. 'I'm DI Bradshaw,' he said, showing his warrant card, and explained why he was there.

'Ah. You need to speak to my wife,' the man said. 'I'll take the kids out so you can talk to Louise in peace and they won't be a nuisance.'

So this was Hugo Wilkins, Colin thought. Despite the initial pleasant smile, he didn't have the same warmth about him as his wife; and it annoyed Colin that Hugo automatically assumed that the children would be a nuisance. Though at least he wasn't just dumping them on the nanny.

'Actually, it would be useful to have a quick chat with you,' Colin said.

Hugo spread his hands and gave a charming smile that didn't reach his eyes. 'I wasn't here when any of this poisoning business happened. I'm afraid I won't be able to help you.'

'Background,' Colin said.

'I'm sure my wife has already told you everything,' Hugo said.

'No harm in confirming things,' Colin said, giving an insincerely charming smile of his own.

'We moved here three years ago, Louise has been busy doing up the mill and setting up the bakery, and I work in London – the commute's unbearable so I live there during the week and I'm home from Friday evening to Monday morning,' Hugo said.

Well, if the man wanted to do an interview on the doorstep, so be it. 'Can you think of anyone who might want to throw suspicion onto your wife or damage the business?' Colin asked, keeping his voice pleasant.

'No. I don't really mix in the village,' Hugo said. 'I have such little time here. Of course I want to spend it with my wife and children rather than other people.'

'Of course,' Colin said. 'And I'm sure you understand that I need to write up my notes of our conversation, then ask you to check it and sign it as being accurate.'

'Leave it with Louise,' Hugo said.

'Can't do that, I'm afraid,' Colin said, knowing that it would annoy the other man. All his instincts told him that Hugo Wilkins was hiding something. Annoying the man just might break that charming persona and give him the gap he was looking for. 'I'll need you to check it and sign it before I leave. Probably better to do it now, before you take the children out.'

Hugo's eyes narrowed, but he didn't argue.

'May I come in?' Colin asked sweetly.

'Oh – I suppose.' Hugo took a step back and called into the house, 'Louise! There's a policeman here. He wants a word.'

'I'll be two minutes!' Louise called.

Colin swiftly wrote up the conversation he'd had with Hugo. The other man scanned it so quickly that Colin wondered whether he'd actually bothered reading it. And why was he so keen to get out of the cottage, away from scrutiny? Or maybe, he thought, the man was just arrogant and expected his wife to handle almost everything while he did whatever he pleased. He remembered

Georgina had said she felt sorry for Louise and that the other woman was struggling with her marriage.

But Hugo duly signed the statement. 'Come on, kids, get a move on!' he called, impatience creeping into his tone.

Sam appeared a moment later, carrying his little sister, while a smaller version of him followed close behind.

'Sorry, DI Bradshaw,' Louise said, coming behind them. 'Hugo, you'd better take Isla's bag with you.'

Hugo rolled his eyes and held his hand out for the bag.

Colin remembered outings with his daughter, Cathy, when she was Isla's age. He'd never forgotten the bag with spare clothes, wipes, a drink and emergency snacks. If he and Marianne had had more than one child, he would never have expected the older child to be in charge of the younger ones, either. He had a feeling that Hugo was the sort who would use his long working hours as an excuse for not engaging with his children, though Colin was pretty sure that his own working hours back when Cathy had been little had been longer than Hugo's and he'd always made time for his daughter.

'Please come in, DI Bradshaw,' Louise said, ushering Colin into the kitchen. 'Can I get you a cup of tea or anything?'

'That's kind of you, but I'm fine,' Colin said.

'This is my mother-in-law, Marion Wilkins,' Louise said, indicating the woman who sat at the kitchen table and who looked very much like her son. 'Marion, this is Detective Inspector Bradshaw. He's been very kind.'

'I'm glad to hear it,' Marion said, 'but I'd rather you put your energies into finding who's behind all this than being *kind*.'

Marion Wilkins was clearly the type of forthright elderly woman who believed in saying exactly what was on her mind, Colin thought. She looked no-nonsense, too, with silver-grey hair in a pixie cut, a strong jaw, and with the kind of expression that would warn would-be muggers not to even *think* about trying to best her. But she made him a cup of tea with swift efficiency, and she was supporting Louise; he knew Georgina would approve of that.

'We're trying to find out who's behind it,' Colin reassured her. 'And you've had no contact from anyone claiming to be behind it, Mrs Wilkins?' he asked Louise.

'No,' she said. 'I don't have a clue who's doing this to me or why. I haven't had any disgruntled customers, I haven't had any difficulties with staff, and nobody seems to be upset that I've restored the mill.' She sighed. 'I just want whoever's doing this to stop and for life to go back to normal. And it's not fair on Billy or his daughter, either. They're under investigation as well.'

'As are their suppliers,' Colin said. 'Sheena did explain to me how campylobacter spreads.'

'Louise knows better than to cut corners or mess about with storage,' Marion said stoutly. 'She's got all her certificates.'

'I know,' Colin said gently. 'I'm not blaming her for any of this.'

'But there'll be plenty who'll point their fingers,' Marion said darkly. 'You know how it is in a village. Word gets round quicker than anything. And what about the kids? It's not very nice for them, at school, people talking about their mum.'

'Indeed,' Colin said. 'I'll level with you, Mrs Wilkins. So far, nobody's contacted Louise to say they're responsible or what they want her to do to make them stop. We have no leads. The same's true for the butchery. Without a motive and without a suspect, we're not going to get very far in the investigation.'

'Hmph,' Marion said, making it clear she didn't think he was doing anywhere near enough.

'If either of you can think of anyone – or any reason why someone might do this – that would be helpful,' Colin said. 'Or maybe your husband? Perhaps it might be worth me talking to him?'

'He isn't here most of the week, so he wouldn't have a clue,' Louise said, echoing what Hugo himself had said.

'What about your nanny?' Colin asked. 'Does she have any thoughts on the situation?'

'No,' Louise said. 'And it's her weekend off.'

'You don't really need her while I'm staying,' Marion said. 'I can help with the kids. And I'm a better cook than she is.'

Louise smiled. 'That's true. But as soon as the ceiling's sorted in your flat, you'll be back in London. I can't really manage the business here and the kids without some help.'

'If you moved back to London,' Marion said, 'you could get rid of Annie. You'd have Hugo home with you every night. And I'd be just round the corner. I could pop round any time you needed me.'

Interesting, Colin thought. Marion Wilkins hadn't just suggested moving back to London, she'd also suggested getting rid of the nanny. Was she simply keen to see her son and grandchildren more regularly, or did she dislike the nanny for some reason? He wondered whether Georgina might be able to shed some light on that particular theory.

'I'm not moving back to London,' Louise said firmly.

It sounded to Colin as if this was a discussion they'd had before, and their positions were entrenched. Marion clearly believed that Louise should sell up and go back to London, whereas Louise wanted very much to stay in Norfolk.

'We'll get through this,' Louise said, lifting her chin. 'The mill and the bakery will be back up and running. Things will sort themselves out.'

'Hmph,' Marion said, making it very clear that she didn't agree.

It was a battle of wills that Colin had no intention of getting in the middle of. 'Thank you for the chat. I'll be in touch.' Just as he'd said to Billy and Sheena, he added, 'If you can think of anything relevant, no matter how obscure or daft it might seem, please let me know.'

'Hmph,' Marion said again.

And Colin was beginning to think that Mrs Wilkins senior might even be a match for Sybbie Walters.

. . .

'OK. I think I've got as much as I can from the diary,' Sybbie said with a sigh. 'Amelia mentions the execution, though she says she didn't go to watch the hanging – she thought it was a terrible thing to treat someone's death as entertainment.'

'Agreed,' Will said.

'She also says in passing that Chorley's Mill was sold to Forrest, but she had no idea what happened to Alfred. William said that until either of the Wenborough mills was run by someone not connected with Herbert Forrest, they'd send the estate's corn further afield for milling,' Sybbie added. 'And I'm proud of Bernard's great-great-great-grandparents for having integrity.'

'I found an obituary for Forrest in the newspapers,' Will said, 'but it's incredibly short. Other obituaries around those years seem to be a bit longer, giving a little bit of detail of what they were known for. Maybe the journalist knew what Forrest was like and didn't want to give him any more publicity. It just says, "Died of apoplexy on July 10, 1865, at Little Wenborough, Herbert Forrest, corn factor and miller, aged 56."'

'Apoplexy. That was what they called a stroke back then,' Georgina said.

'There was nothing in the papers about Catherine Forrest or Alfred Chorley,' Will said. 'Maybe they weren't important enough for the press to report on them.'

'What did you find in the parish records, Georgie?' Sybbie asked.

'Catherine Forrest died a year after Daniel,' Georgina said. 'There's a note in the parish register that says the vicar thinks she died of a broken heart after her son's death. She was buried in the churchyard at Little Wenborough. And I'm sorry to say that Alfred Chorley died from cholera in February 1849, in the workhouse at Wicklewood, along with several other inmates in the infirmary.'

'So the dementia didn't kill him,' Will said. 'And you were right that he ended up in the workhouse.'

'In their hospital,' Georgina said. 'But how sad. Margaret tried so hard to keep him safe and looked after.'

'We know from Will's newspaper search that Forrest lived until 1865,' Sybbie said.

'And the cause of death was a stroke. He was buried at Little Wenborough, though there's no comment in the parish records. I looked through the civil records, and there's no record of him marrying again after Catherine's death, and him having any more children,' Georgina said. 'So who was his heir?'

'And what happened to all the mills?' Sybbie asked.

Will glanced at his watch. 'Bea will be up, but she won't be at the theatre yet,' he said. 'She'll know the most likely scenario and where to look.' When Bea wasn't acting, she worked for a probate genealogy company.

A quick phone call netted him the information they wanted. 'She says inheritance worked pretty much the same way as it does today,' Will reported. 'If Forrest died without a will and without heirs, his property would be considered "bona vacantia", or "without owners", so by law it would pass to the Crown. The Treasury solicitors would put notices in *The London Gazette* to check for any possible heirs, and if nobody replied they'd administer the estate, settle the debts and collect the remaining assets. She says you can search *The Gazette*, as it's called now, to find the notices.' His phone beeped with a text. 'Good old Bea. She's just sent me a link.'

He brought up the website on his laptop, and tapped Herbert Forrest's name into the search box.

'Here we go. Herbert Forrest, deceased,' Will said. 'It's in the 30 January 1866 edition.'

Georgina and Sybbie read the notice over his shoulder.

Notice is hereby given that all creditors and other persons having any claim or demand on or against the estate of Herbert Forrest, of Little Wenborough, in the county of Norfolk, corn factor and miller (who died intestate on the 10th day of July 1865, and of whose estate and effect letters of administration were granted on the 17th day of January 1866), are hereby required to send in the particulars of their claims and demand upon the estate of the deceased to me the undersigned, James Mason, the administrator of the deceased, at the Mill House, Mill Street, Little Wenborough in the County of Norfolk, on or before the 30th day of April 1866, or in default thereof the said administrator will at the expiration of that time proceed to administer the estate and distribute the assets of the deceased among the parties entitled that, having regards to the claims of demands only of which he shall have had notice; and will not be liable to any person of his claim he shall not have had noticed at the time of such distribution; and all persons indebted to the estate of the deceased are hereby required to pay the amount of their respective debts, and to deliver up any property of the deceased to me, forthwith – dated this 26th day of January 1866. James Mason, administrator.

'Until Doris gets back to us,' Georgina said with a sigh, 'we're pretty much stuck at the moment. We have nowhere else to look.'

'Then I shall love you and leave you, and talk Bernard into having lunch out,' Sybbie said. 'Let me know if Doris finds out more.'

'Will do.'

Before she left, Sybbie made a brief fuss of Bert, who managed a couple of wan wags of his tail.

Georgina glanced at her watch. 'I know it's Saturday, but I have no idea when Colin's going to be back. Normally I would have suggested we could go out for lunch and potter round the city for the afternoon, but I don't want to leave Bert on his own.'

'Of course you don't,' Will said. 'Let's just have a quiet afternoon here, though I might go out for some fresh air a bit later on.' He gave her a rueful smile. 'I'm sorry we didn't get very far with Margaret's case this morning.'

'We know a bit more than we did,' Georgina said. 'Hopefully what we found will help jog Margaret's memory, and we'll get another lead.'

'I can see why you and Sybbie enjoy working on the cold cases,' Will said. 'It's so interesting, having a window into the past – very sad, too, but fascinating.'

'Hopefully we can find a way of clearing Margaret's name,' Georgina said. 'Right – time for lunch, I think...'

Colin came home later that afternoon. Bert managed a waggy tail to greet him, though not his usual pattery, bouncing dance of welcome. Colin bent to make a fuss of him, then kissed Georgina. 'Sorry I've been so long.' He glanced at her laptop on the table. 'No Will?'

'Out for a w-word to clear his head. Bert's not quite up to joining him,' Georgina said.

'Though he is looking a bit more like himself,' Colin said, ruffling the top of the dog's head.

'You look as if you could do with a coffee,' Georgina said.

'And a biscuit,' Colin said, looking hopeful.

Not when he'd admitted to what his blood sugar levels were at his last blood test. Georgina raised her eyebrows. 'You're really asking for illicit substances?'

Colin sighed and gave her a hug. 'No. And thank you for being the Biscuit Police. Sorry. I'm just...' He grimaced and shook his head.

'Frustrated, by the look of you,' Georgina said, stroking his hair back from his forehead. 'How did it go with Louise and Billy?' she asked.

'I'm really at a loss with this one,' Colin said. 'I don't know which of them is the target of the poisoner. Nobody's sent either of them a threatening note, and neither of them can think of anyone who might hold a grudge against them. There's nothing to go on.'

'I've been thinking,' Georgina said. 'This might be a bit of a long shot, but Louise's husband isn't happy in Norfolk.'

'Mmm – he definitely didn't want to talk to me and made it clear he didn't think he could be helpful,' Colin said. 'Until I explained otherwise.'

'You met him?'

'Very briefly. He was just about to take the children out when I arrived.'

'What's he like?' Georgina asked, curious.

'I only met him briefly,' Colin repeated. 'And took a very short statement from him.'

'But you formed an opinion.'

Colin grimaced. 'Let's just say he's not my sort of person. And he doesn't really seem to fit with Louise. She's warm and welcoming.'

'And he's snooty?'

'Merchant banker,' Colin said.

Georgina grinned. 'Colin Bradshaw. Are you using Cockney rhyming slang?'

'No comment,' Colin said, but he grinned back. 'All right, I didn't like him.'

'Hmm.' She paused. 'Could he perhaps be behind the poisonings?'

'What would his motive be?' Colin asked.

'If Louise's business fails,' Georgina said, 'she might be more receptive to moving the whole family back to London, and he won't have to trek down to Norfolk and back every week.'

'It's a theory,' Colin said, 'but we can't make accusations without evidence, and there's no evidence that Hugo had anything to do with the poisoning. Plus there are two different types of poison involved. Miss Hurst died from eating a sausage roll laced with rat poison, whereas everyone else who's been ill – including Valerie Waring and Bert – has been affected by campylobacter. Why would someone use two different forms of poison?'

'Maybe there are two different poisoners,' Georgina suggested.

'It's a bit of a coincidence that they both struck at exactly the same time,' Colin said.

'And you don't like coincidences. I know.' She sighed. 'We're missing something.'

'A suspect and a motive, for starters,' Colin said. 'I met Louise's mother-in-law, too. She's very protective of Louise and she took me to task for not finding out who did it.'

'That's a bit unfair on you, but I'm glad Louise has some support,' Georgina said.

'Up to a point. Marion Wilkins also thinks that they should all move back to London,' Colin said. 'Though I think that's probably because she wants to see more of the grandchildren.'

'Did you see the nanny?' Georgina asked.

'No. She was off duty. Have you met her?' Colin asked.

'No. Though Jodie doesn't like her – she says Annie Newman is a bit snooty,' Georgina said. 'Which isn't me suggesting that Annie's a potential suspect, just that I think Louise is struggling a bit. She's trying to protect the kids from the worst of it and hasn't had a lot of support from her husband or the nanny.'

'Sadly I think your assessment is spot-on,' Colin said. 'How are you getting on with Margaret Chorley's case?'

Georgina brought him up to speed with the research she'd done with Sybbie and Will, and showed him the evidence they had so far. 'We can probably discount most of what's written in the broadside, because they were all about making money for the printer and giving the audience a mixture of entertainment and moral education,' she said. 'The little boy wasn't supposed to eat the cake. It's pretty clear that his death was accidental.'

'And the intended recipient of the poisoned flour was Forrest's wife?' Colin asked.

'That was the prosecution's argument, but Margaret's character was definitely smeared in court,' Georgina said. 'The witnesses lied. They claimed they saw her consorting with Forrest, insinuating that firstly she was free with her sexual favours – which was really frowned upon at the time – and secondly that she knew Forrest was already married but was trying to snare him anyway. That would have prejudiced some of the jury against her, and possibly the judge as well. And then the witnesses claimed they heard her say she was going to get rid of Forrest's wife so he could marry her.'

'Then the poisoned flour arrived at the house, which was apparently targeted at Forrest's wife, so the argument was that Margaret must have been responsible for sending it,' Colin said.

'Exactly,' Georgina said. 'But there are so many inconsistencies. Firstly, Margaret was incredibly busy keeping her father's business going while he was unable to work. When would she have had the time to take a parcel of flour over to Forrest's house in the next village? Secondly, she already used arsenic in the mill to get rid of vermin, and she bought it from the village pharmacist in Great Wenborough. Why would she go to a completely different village to buy arsenic from a different supplier, instead of using what she already had to hand? Thirdly, it doesn't fit in with her character that she'd try to murder an invalid, when her own father was mentally fragile and she was doing her best to look after him. Or that she would have deliberately poisoned a child. Will says a lot of deaths by poison back then were accidental rather than murder, and that was one of the reasons why the industry needed to be regulated.' She shook her head. 'What I don't understand is why nobody testified in Margaret's favour. No neighbours, no friends. It seems *odd*. Especially as Amelia's diary hints that Chorley's Mill was popular because Margaret and her dad were honest, whereas Forrest would cheat you as soon as look at you.'

'How much influence did Forrest have locally, as a business owner?' Colin asked.

'He owned several mills,' Georgina said, 'as well as a corn dealing business. So he would probably have had quite a few employees in the area.'

'Given that he comes across as a difficult character, I think the men who worked for Forrest were unlikely to stand up in court and speak out against him, because they knew there would be repercussions afterwards,' Colin said. 'And we have to bear in mind the social structure at the time. A woman's testimony would have been ruled out as being biased – as women sticking together – or generally seen as less significant than a man's. Even if a neighbour or friend had testified in her favour, it would more than likely have been discounted. Which I know is atrocious, but that's how things were back then.' He frowned. 'Do we have any solid facts about what happened?'

'The presence of arsenic,' Georgina said. 'A pharmacist tested the contents of the little boy's stomach and the results showed there was arsenic, so we know the poison must have been in the ingredients used to make the cake. It was most likely in the flour, because the prosecution's lawyer did a bit of grandstanding in court and flung some of the flour from the parcel into the fire. The paper reported that everyone in the courtroom could smell garlic.'

'Garlic?' Colin asked.

Georgina explained about arsine gas smelling of garlic when heated.

'OK. So there was definitely poison in the flour, and the little boy ate the cake baked with that flour. But how do we know who actually put the arsenic in the flour?' Colin asked.

'We don't. Though Will, Sybbie and I have a couple of theories. Maybe it was Forrest himself. Perhaps he was fed up with having a wife who was an invalid, and wanted to marry someone younger – someone who might give him more children and might also come with a nice fat dowry,' Georgina said. 'Or maybe it was the housekeeper, who was fond of Catherine Forrest and thought that Catherine's status as an invalid might be linked to her husband's behaviour.' At Colin's raised eyebrow, she explained, 'If Forrest died, then he wouldn't be able to treat his wife badly, and she might recover.'

'Both of them had a motive, the method and the opportunity,' Colin said.

'Or maybe Catherine and the housekeeper planned it between them, if Catherine had had enough of her husband's behaviour and was friends with the housekeeper,' Georgina said. 'Or it could even have been one of Forrest's other employees – someone he'd bullied, and they finally snapped and wanted to get back at him.'

'Let's backtrack a bit. So your main theories are that either Forrest poisoned the flour because he wanted to get rid of his invalid wife, or Catherine and the housekeeper poisoned the flour to get rid of Forrest. The flour was delivered in a parcel which said it was for Catherine. If Forrest was the one who sent the parcel, the housekeeper wouldn't have known the flour was poisoned. So why did she make a cake instead of using it for Catherine's drink?' Colin asked.

'That wasn't asked in court. And it's also why I'm leaning towards the idea that Catherine and – *or* – the housekeeper was behind the poison rather than Forrest. Supposing the parcel was left out and Forrest saw it? Instead of thinking that someone was being kind to his wife, he decided it was his – because the laws of the time meant everything she owned before the marriage belonged to him as soon as that ring was on her finger. We know Forrest was avaricious, because he was trying to buy Chorley's mill for a knock-down price and he'd been accused of cheating in business. The housekeeper and Catherine would have known his likely reaction, which was to demand that the flour was used for his benefit rather than Catherine's,' Georgina said. 'If Forrest had been behind the poison, surely he would have encouraged the housekeeper to use it for Catherine's drink instead of telling her to make a cake with it?'

'It's also possible that the housekeeper might have added the arsenic to the flour after Forrest told her to use it. Hmm. Did the housekeeper testify at the trial?' Colin asked.

'No. Apparently she was too affected by the child's death and had sunk into a depression. She was in an asylum, being treated,' Georgina said. 'And Catherine was too unwell to come to court to testify.'

'That's rather convenient,' Colin said.

'Isn't it just?' Georgina asked.

'So where do you go from here?'

'I don't know,' Georgina said with a sigh. 'At the moment, I'm as stuck as you, because I can't prove my theory. Margaret was buried at the castle in an unmarked grave and there are no bones to find at the mill; besides, Bert isn't well enough to find anything. I was wondering whether I could trace the housekeeper and see if there was anything in the asylum records – that is, if they're not closed.'

'This all happened nearly two hundred years ago. Even if you assume the housekeeper was young and lived to a hundred, you should be safely outside the timespan for records to be closed,' Colin said.

'That's my next move,' Georgina said. 'But also, there are rumours of things being moved at the mill.' She glanced at his expression and sighed inwardly. 'Which isn't me trying to convince you that poltergeists exist. But Doris did say that Margaret has been trying to remember something she left at the mill. I'm wondering whether Louise might have found it during the restoration. Letters, a diary, or something like that. I want to ask her about it.'

'I don't need to ask you to be careful,' Colin said.

'I won't interfere in your case, if that's what you mean,' Georgina said. 'Though I have a feeling that someone's framing Louise, just as someone framed Margaret Chorley. The question is – who?'

ELEVEN

Colin made some coffee while Georgina rang Louise. 'This is a bit of an odd question,' Georgina said, 'but I was wondering – when you restored the mill, did you come across any documents?'

'What sort of documents?' Louise asked.

'I'm not sure,' Georgina admitted. 'Letters, perhaps, or a diary. Or maybe something in with the deeds.'

'The deeds had a plan of the grounds and the buildings, but all the letters seemed to be mainly legal correspondence about transferring the title,' Louise said.

'You don't remember seeing anything about Margaret Chorley?' Georgina asked.

'No, but I can get them out and have another look through them,' Louise said. 'Did you manage to find out any more about her?'

'We've been through the newspaper reports of her trial,' Georgina said, 'and we're pretty sure she was framed by the man who then bought the mill from her dad at a ridiculous price. We're not sure who was really behind the poisoning and whether the target was Herbert Forrest or his wife, but it definitely suited Forrest for Margaret to take the blame because she was the obstacle to him buying the mill. The murder charge – and her execution – removed that obstacle.' She filled Louise in on the findings.

'That's all so sad,' Louise said. 'You really think you can prove she was innocent?'

'Yes,' Georgina said.

'But at the time she was blamed for something she hadn't done. Just as people are pointing the finger at me for something I haven't done.' Louise bit her lip. 'I just hope that I don't have to leave Great Wenborough under a cloud.'

'I'm very much doubt that,' Georgina said. 'Colin's good at his job.'

'Without a suspect or a motive, how's he ever going to find out who was responsible for the poisonings?' Louise asked, and she sounded as if she had the entire weight of the world on her shoulders.

'The case will break,' Georgina said. 'Sometimes it takes a while, but Colin *will* get a lead and your name will be cleared, I'm sure of it.'

'Thank you,' Louise said. 'I'll have a look through those papers and get back to you.'

On Sunday morning, Louise knocked on Georgina's door. 'I found something,' she said. 'It was a little book I found tucked behind a brick at the bottom of the ground floor of the windmill – which we thought used to be the office. How nobody found it before us, I don't know. It's been a bit nibbled round the edges by mice, and it's not very easy to read the handwriting – I'm afraid I gave up – but I think it might be a diary. And I brought the deeds over, too, in case you spot something that I've missed.'

'Thank you. That's amazing,' Georgina said.

'I'd forgotten all about the book, to be honest,' Louise said. 'I found it fairly early on after we moved here, but I was working all hours on the restoration and I put it with the deeds, intending to take a proper look at it later. Except I never had the time and then it just slipped my mind.'

'I've done a fair bit of work with old letters and diaries now, so I've got quite used to Victorian handwriting,' Georgina said. 'I'll try and transcribe it for you. Do you want to come in for a cup of tea, or something?'

Louise shook her head. 'I'd better get back to the kids. I've left them with Hugo, and he's—' She stopped, as if catching herself. 'Well, he's had a tough week. A lot of travelling. He needs a break.'

You've had a tough week, too, Georgina thought. You could do with a break. And if Colin doesn't like your husband, that makes me think he's probably a selfish bloke who doesn't deserve you. But she didn't say anything, not wanting to make Louise feel worse.

'Thanks for all you're doing,' Louise finished, looking slightly sad. 'I'll wait to hear from you.'

'I'll be in touch as soon as I've got something to tell you,' Georgina promised.

When Louise left, Georgina went back into the kitchen, where Colin was reading the paper and Will appeared to be looking at job vacancies on his laptop.

'That was Louise,' she said. 'She brought the deeds over – and what she thinks might be a diary belonging to Margaret Chorley. She says it's been nibbled by mice and some of the pages are loose, but luckily it didn't get damp – which is quite surprising, given that it was hidden behind some loose bricks.'

'Are you planning to work on it for the whole day?' Colin asked. 'Only I could do with some sea air to clear my head. Given that Bert seems a lot brighter this morning, I thought maybe he would enjoy a trip out.'

'Actually, I'd be up for that, too,' Will said. 'If I'm invited.'

Colin smiled. 'Of course you are.'

'Thanks. And I'll cook dinner for us this evening,' Will said.

'That sounds perfect,' Georgina said. 'Let's take a really quick look at the diary to see what kind of state it's in, and then we'll go.' She opened the folder and took out the documents. The deeds were tied in a bundle, but the diary was at the front: a small volume about twelve centimetres by seventeen, with a dark leather cover that had definitely been chewed by mice. She opened it carefully; as Louise had warned her, some of the pages were loose, where the stitches holding them together had worn away, and others were nibbled at the edges. The writing was in brown ink, and was tiny; unlike Amelia, Margaret hadn't left margins on either side of the page. She'd drawn a line between each entry but clearly hadn't used a ruler to do it.

'I'm going to need a daylight lamp and I'll have to photograph every page so I can enlarge it before I start to transcribe this,' Georgina said. 'Margaret's handwriting isn't quite as clear as Amelia's.'

'It looks more like a doctor's handwriting,' Colin agreed. 'And she probably wrote last thing at night, by the light of a candle, which wouldn't have helped.'

'Probably not even a wax candle, because they were expensive,' Georgina said. 'Tallow candles give a duller light.'

'And notebooks weren't cheap, so she'd keep her writing tiny to make the notebook last,' Will said. 'I guess at least she's only written one way across the page. One of my old housemates from uni is a historian, and he said in Regency times when they got to the end of the page when they were writing a personal letter, they used to turn it ninety degrees and treat it as if it were another sheet of paper.'

Georgina winced. 'That would *definitely* be easier to read in daylight rather than candlelight. Especially if the ink bled through the paper.' She looked at the first page of the diary. 'This seems to be from 1844.'

'The year before the trial,' Will said.

Georgina nodded. 'Hopefully it will give us some more places to look for evidence. But let's go out now, and I'll do the photography when we get back.'

· · ·

Wells-next-the-Sea on the north Norfolk coast was one of Georgina's favourite places in the world. Even though it was cold and a bit windy, she loved walking through the beach huts and over the dunes across the sand, listening to the sea swish onto the shore. As the tide had ebbed, the sea had left rippled marks on the sand, and an array of shells were scattered across them: razor clam shells looking like an old-fashioned cut-throat razor, fan-shaped ribbed cockle shells, and tiny Baltic tellin shells with their yellow, pink and white bands. Bert walked between Georgina and Colin, making sure they were both kept in his sight as he pattered along the sand.

'He's still a bit clingy – not quite back to his old self, just yet,' Will said, and ruffled the fur on the top of the spaniel's head. 'Poor boy.'

They stopped after a quarter of an hour so Georgina could give Bert a drink in the portable water-bowl she kept in the backpack she used on longer walks, and then walked on towards Holkham Bay. The sound of the waves against the sand was soothing, and Georgina hoped it would act like a kind of white noise to distract them while their brains worked on the puzzle of who was framing Louise, and who was really responsible for the poisoning of little Daniel Forrest.

Finally they headed back to the car, buying coffee from the little café on the way to warm themselves up again.

'Definitely no more cobwebs,' Will said with a smile. 'Thanks for bringing me.'

'I think the walk did me good, too,' Georgina said. She clipped Bert into his harness on the back seat, and Will sat beside him.

'What about you?' she asked Colin softly. 'Has it helped?'

'It's made me feel better, but I'm still stuck,' Colin said. 'Louise hasn't had any anonymous letters warning her off, nobody's approached her to sell the business, and she can't remember upsetting anyone. But there were two separate instances of campylobacter poisoning – the one that affected the children, and the one affecting the wider customers.'

'The one that killed Valerie,' Georgina said.

Colin nodded. 'One, you could consider an accident or maybe bad luck. Two feels deliberate. Plus there's the rat poison that killed Miss Hurst. Without a motive, I can't pinpoint a suspect – which leaves me with Louise herself, or Billy. Neither of them has a motive. Why would they destroy their own businesses? Billy's butchery has been in the family for decades, and he's looking forward to his daughter taking over when he retires. Louise worked crazy hours to restore that mill and clearly loves the place. It doesn't make sense.' He shook his head. 'The crime scene team haven't turned up anything, either. All we have are the lab results identifying the poison and the vehicle for said poison. "What", "when" and "how" isn't enough. We need to know "who" and "why".'

'Put it to the back of your mind and let your brain puzzle it out,' Georgina suggested. 'And, given that your case has similarities with mine – both poisonings and both potentially framing someone innocent – maybe something will come out of that diary to spark off a lead for your case as well as mine.'

Back at the Rookery Farm, Colin caught up with some of his paperwork in Georgina's office while Will prepared dinner in the kitchen, and Georgina photographed each page of the diary on the dining room table with the help of a daylight lamp.

'This is all really sad,' Doris said, reading over Georgina's shoulder as she photographed the diary. 'Margaret is chronicling her father's gradual decline – how he's forgetting how to do things he's always been able to do, and she's having to do them for him. How sometimes he looks at her as if he can't remember who she is. He keeps calling her by her mum's name.'

'I've found that with my own mum,' Georgina said quietly. 'She can remember things so clearly from years back, but she can't remember what she had for breakfast that morning. Bea pops in to see her as often as she can, but it's not fair to put the burden on her. I'd like to move Mum to Norwich when she starts needing more care, but then again that's going to make it really hard for her friends to see her and she'd miss them.' She sighed. 'The sheltered accommodation manager keeps me up to date with everything, but I know it isn't enough.'

'What's the alternative?' Doris asked. 'If you moved back to London now, would you be happy?'

'Well – no,' Georgina admitted. 'I've settled here. I'm happy. I like my life. But I still need to do more for my mum. A monthly visit isn't anywhere near enough. I need to juggle things better. Especially as she won't be around forever.'

'If I could give you a physical hug, I would,' Doris said.

'I know. And I appreciate it,' Georgina said.

'Do you think the diary might be what Margaret's been looking for?' Doris asked.

'Perhaps. I'm going to start transcribing it tomorrow,' Georgina said. 'I messaged Sybbie to let her know about this, and she's coming over to help tomorrow. And Will's here. Between the three of us, we should be able to sort it out.' She paused. 'Did Margaret have any views on our theories about who the poisoner was – Forrest himself, Catherine or the housekeeper?'

'She thinks Catherine would have been too scared of him to risk trying to poison him. She thinks it's more likely that Forrest tried to frame her, with Catherine as the intended victim, but it went wrong. What she can't work out is why the housekeeper made a cake with the flour instead of the pap for Catherine,' Doris said. 'What about Louise? Has Colin worked out who's trying to frame her?'

'There are no suspects and no motives, so far,' Georgina said.

'The sea air didn't quite do the trick, then?' Doris asked wryly.

'Not this time,' Georgina agreed.

'You're both good at reading Victorian handwriting,' Will said, the middle of the following morning, when Sybbie had sat down at Georgina's kitchen table with a mug of coffee. 'So why don't you read the diary out loud, page by page, and I'll type it up as you talk?'

'Are you sure you don't mind?' Georgina asked.

'I'm invested in this now,' Will said. 'I want to know who really poisoned the flour. I also want to know if there's a way of proving that Forrest framed Margaret, so she can get a posthumous pardon.'

'I'm with you, dear boy,' Sybbie said with a smile.

Between them, they went through the diary, detailing Margaret's worries about her father's health and how she'd consulted a doctor who could only suggest letting blood, dosing him with opium or purging him with senna and rhubarb to calm excitement. Or, as a final resort, admitting him to the county asylum as a pauper lunatic.

'To be fair,' Will said, 'medics didn't really understand dementia back then. They called it "senile dementia", but they were still working on outdated theories of the four humours and what have you.'

'Margaret didn't want to put her dad in an asylum. She said she didn't want to hide him away, or leave him somewhere that might not treat him as kindly as she would. She paid their neighbour, Harriet Rowlands, to sit with him while she was working, and then she looked after him herself once she'd finished at the mill,' Sybbie said. 'And it sounds as if the families of the people they employed also helped – Harriet helped with the laundry, and the cart driver's wife made dinner for them both.'

'Alfred was clearly well-loved in the community, and it looks as if Margaret was, too. So why didn't any of them stand up for her at the trial and give her a character reference?' Georgina asked.

'Because Forrest threatened them,' Doris said. 'He said if anyone took her part in court, he'd sack every member of their family in his employ and make sure they couldn't get another job. He'd say he caught them thieving, and Lord Rutherford would indict anyone he put in front of him.'

'I can see how that would be a deterrent,' Georgina said, after filling the others in on Doris's comments. 'But other local magistrates knew that Forrest was dishonest. William Walters certainly didn't trust him. Surely he could have spoken up?'

'It would have been one person's word against another,' Sybbie said. 'Even if the judges knew that Rutherford was corrupt, without proof they couldn't have backed William's word against his.'

They carried on working their way through the diary. In the pages, Margaret described Forrest cornering her at the Red Lion, and mentioned witnesses. She also told her neighbour Harriet about it; Harriet said she'd send her husband, Jack, to fetch the beer for Alfred in future, to make sure Margaret stayed out of Forrest's clutches.

The day that Forrest suggested buying the mill, Margaret was totally outraged – even more so when she complained to Rutherford and he did nothing to help her. *'They are in league, and there is nothing I can do about it. What is the word of a young, unmarried woman worth? Nothing, when it's measured against the lies of a married man,'* Georgina read.

And Margaret sounded genuinely shocked to hear of the death of Daniel Forrest. *'I can think of a great many who would be happy to see Herbert Forrest dead. The farmers he has cheated, the workers he has bullied, and his poor invalid wife Catherine. But who in the Lord's name would kill a child?'* Sybbie read. *'It must surely have been an accident and the cake must have been meant for his father. His poor mother. This will not help her recover from her illness.'*

The final entry in the diary addressed Forrest's claims that Margaret was the one who had sent the poisoned flour to his home.

'I wish I had thought of it, but if I had poisoned the flour, I would have made sure that Forrest was the one to eat the poison, not the little boy,' Georgina read. *'He has no proof, because I did not do it. I fear he is behind it all. I believe he sent the flour to poison his wife and get rid of her, because he has lost patience with being married to an invalid. By claiming that I am the one who did it, he thinks they will put me in Norwich prison until the Assizes. I will be out of his way and he can take the mill from my father, and by the*

time the judge hears the case, sees I am innocent and lets me go, it will be too late to stop him.'

'What a horrible position to be in,' Sybbie said. 'And listen to this next bit. She clearly feels completely alone in the world, even though she knows she has friends. *'I did not kill Daniel Forrest. I never tried to kill anybody. I cannot ask Lord Rutherford for help, because I know he is in league with Forrest. I cannot ask Lord Wyatt for help, because he is the magistrate of Little Wenborough, not Great Wenborough. I cannot ask my friends and neighbours for help, because Forrest will be set against anyone who tries to help me and he will make sure they lose their jobs and their homes. All I can do is ask the vicar to pray for me, and trust to God that the truth will come out.'*

'The truth didn't come out, though, did it? At least, not back then. I wonder if there's anything in the vicar's papers?' Georgina said.

'And could the vicar have stood up for Margaret against Forrest?' Will asked. 'Or could Forrest have had the vicar sacked?'

'Forrest could have complained about the vicar to Rutherford, who probably had the gift of the living for the local vicar – which means he could suggest who the next vicar could be once the current vicar decided to move on. But only the bishop could actually remove the vicar, and there would have to be a good reason for doing it,' Sybbie said.

'If the vicar stayed, Forrest could have made his life difficult,' Will said thoughtfully.

'I think we need to look at the local archives,' Georgina said. 'We can check if anything was deposited by the vicar's family, or by Margaret's neighbours. Especially Harriet Rowlands, the one who helped her.'

'Margaret's dad ran a mill, so he needed to be able to read and write for the sake of the business – and as Margaret was helping him, she would have needed to be literate as well,' Will said. 'But most of her neighbours would have been agricultural labourers.

How many of them went to school and knew how to read and write?'

'In the first half of the nineteenth century, not that many,' Sybbie said. 'But by the middle of the century, a lot of churches were running Sunday schools, and in 1870 there was the Education Act which set up school boards to build and manage schools in areas where there weren't any. The problem was, the parents couldn't afford to pay school fees – or to lose their children's wages. And education wasn't compulsory at that point.'

'So even if children were supposed to go to school, most of the time they didn't,' Will said. 'The chances are, we're not going to have anything written down from Harriet. Maybe her children wrote something down, but that's a long shot.'

'We can still look,' Georgina said. 'Road trip, tomorrow?'

'Works for me,' Sybbie said. 'I have an Archives Card. I'll give you the details if you need them to book our seats.'

'I'd like to come, too,' Will said, 'except I don't have an Archives Card.'

'It's an online application,' Georgina said. 'As long as you have some ID, we can organise that now, and then I'll book our session.'

'Sounds like the perfect plan,' Will said.

TWELVE

On Tuesday morning, Georgina, Sybbie and Will went to the Records Office – a modern building on the outskirts of the city where the county's archives were kept. Once Will had finalised his Archives Card so he was able to access the search room, the three of them spent the morning talking to one of the archivists about the quest to find the truth about Margaret Chorley, and also showed her Margaret's diary. Georgina promised to send over the files with Will's transcript and the photographed pages.

Sadly, there were no papers for the Chorley's Mill or for any businesses in Great Wenborough for the relevant time period, there were no relevant personal papers, and there was nothing marked in the margins of the parish records either.

'The best thing I can suggest now is asking for help on social media,' the archivist said. 'Someone who's looked into their family history might have some information to shed light on the case – and people love sharing their family history and feeling they're helping to solve a mystery,' she added with a smile.

'Thank you for spending so much time with us,' Georgina said.

'My pleasure. Good luck. And do keep me posted if someone contacts you with anything helpful,' the archivist said.

. . .

Later that afternoon, Jodie dropped in with Harry, who was happy to make a quiet fuss of Bert while his mum talked to Georgina.

'Harry's a bit upset,' she confided. 'He's become really friendly with Sam Wilkins. They did football training together on Saturday mornings, and since the whole class was ill, Harry's been... well, not himself. It took him until this afternoon to tell me what's wrong. It seems Sam's worried that he'll have to leave Little Wenborough and go back to London.'

'Why?' Georgina asked, surprised. 'Is Louise talking about giving up the business, then?' Yet Louise had been determined not to let the person trying to frame her win. What a shame that the young woman was going to be driven out of the mill by the unknown poisoner, just as Margaret Chorley had been driven out by the person who'd framed her.

'I don't really know,' Jodie said. 'According to Harry, Sam's parents have been arguing a lot. You know Sam's gran – his dad's mum – is staying with them while her flat's being sorted out.'

'There was a leak and they found asbestos in her ceiling,' Georgina said, remembering what Louise had told her.

Jodie winced. 'That'll take a fair bit of sorting out. Anyway, it seems Sam's gran agrees with his dad that they all ought to leave Norfolk and go back to London. Sam says he overheard his dad saying to his mum that if she wanted to stay here, he'd take her to court for custody of the kids because he wants them back in London with him. Sam's so upset about that. He doesn't want to leave his mum, and he's pretty sure Noah and Isla want to stay here with her, too. He thinks if they end up back in London without their mum, they'll be stuck with the nanny all the time, because his dad works really long hours.' Jodie lowered her voice. 'I wouldn't mind betting that includes going to the pub every night after work for champagne. Beer wouldn't be good enough for the likes of him.'

'I take it you don't like Hugo very much?' Georgina asked.

Jodie shook her head. 'Louise, she's all right. She's down to earth. Normal. Hugo is...' She paused, clearly unsure how to phrase it. 'I mean, even his *name* is posh. I don't know what Louise sees in him. He's not even that good-looking – his eyes are that pale sort of blue that would give anyone the creeps – but he really fancies himself. And he's useless with the kids. I can't see him taking the boys to the Rec to kick a football about, or pushing Isla on the swing.'

Colin hadn't warmed to Hugo, either, Georgina remembered. 'Maybe he'll connect more with them when they're a bit older,' Georgina said.

'I'm not so sure. He doesn't even come to football training at the weekend, like most of the dads do. And the way your two talk about their dad – it's obvious they idolised him, and he'd always make time for them even though he had a really busy job,' Jodie said. 'Whereas I don't think Hugo gives his kids a second thought. The worst thing is, it looks like his mum is taking his side. And apparently the nanny wants to go back to London, too.'

'Meanwhile, Louise wants to stay here and the kids are stuck in the middle? That's a horrible situation for all of them,' Georgina said.

'Harry's upset because his friend's upset and he doesn't know what to say to him. I'm not really sure what to tell him to say to Sam, either,' Jodie admitted. 'It sounds as if Louise and her husband are trying not to let the kids know how rocky things are between them, but Sam hasn't been sleeping so well since he's been sleeping on the camp bed, and obviously he hears the fights late at night.'

'Maybe just tell Harry – who'll no doubt pass it on to Sam – that sometimes adults struggle to sort things out, just like kids do in the playground, and shouting doesn't necessarily mean the worst is going to happen,' Georgina suggested. 'Funny, I had the impression from Louise that her mother-in-law was a lot more supportive than her husband. But you say she's taking Hugo's side? Maybe I got my wires crossed, then.'

'I hope I'm the one who got it wrong,' Jodie said. 'But when I met Marion – Louise's mother-in-law – she came across to me as one of those who like to tell you their opinion, and they feel they have the right to say whatever they like just because they're old. You know the sort – the type who doesn't put herself in someone else's shoes and think how they might feel before she opens her mouth.' She shook her head. '*Families*. I was heartbroken when Harry's dad did a runner to the other side of the world when I was pregnant, but I think now maybe he did me a favour, after all. I don't get any hassle, and me and Harry are doing all right. I'm really lucky with my family and friends.'

'Poor Louise. What with the poisonings, having to close the business temporarily, and now her husband wanting her to sell up and just forget about all the hard work she put into the mill – that's tough,' Georgina said sympathetically.

'She said you were looking into the murder that happened there a couple of hundred years ago,' Jodie said.

Georgina filled her friend in on Margaret Chorley's case.

'That stinks,' Jodie said. 'Surely the judge could see it was a put-up job?'

'Sadly not,' Georgina said. 'Will and I have spent this afternoon putting things up on social media, asking if anyone has looked into their family history and found any connection with the Chorleys, the Forrests or anyone who was a witness to some of what happened but didn't give evidence. It might be that someone, somewhere has something written down. Letters, a diary. Something. *Anything*.' Georgina spread her hands.

'And Doris hasn't managed to get you any more information?'

'She told us Margaret was looking for something, and Louise found a diary. Though I'm not sure it's enough to get a review of the case and a posthumous pardon. But I agree with you – it really does stink that there were witnesses but they didn't give any evidence.'

'Do you think the judge was paid off?' Jodie asked.

'No. I think Forrest intimidated the witnesses, telling them to keep their mouths shut or they would lose their jobs and he would spread the word that they were unreliable, so they wouldn't get another job very easily.' She sighed. 'That's why we took the archivist's suggestion of asking for help on social media. Keeping quiet about someone doing wrong when you know you should have spoken up is the sort of thing that would prey on someone's mind towards the end of their life. Even if they couldn't write things down in 1845, maybe by thirty years later they might have learned to write, or at the very least they would have children or grandchildren who could write things down for them.'

'Let me know how you get on – and if I can do anything,' Jodie said. 'I'd better get Harry home for his tea. Thanks for the chat, and the advice.'

'Any time,' Georgina said, meaning it.

'What Jodie was saying about Louise's mother-in-law – Harrison's mum was a bit like that,' Doris said when Jodie had gone.

'Like what?' Georgina asked.

'Thinking she could say anything she liked – though it wasn't because she was old, it was because she thought herself the social superior to all her neighbours,' Doris said.

'Irene was a nasty piece of work, full stop. But Louise sounds as if she's quite fond of her mother-in-law,' Georgina said thoughtfully.

'Look like th'innocent flower/ But be the serpent under't,' Doris quoted.

Georgina knew the quote well. 'You think that's what Louise's mother-in-law is doing? Pretending to support her, but actually undermining her?'

'Think about it,' Doris said. 'There weren't any cases of people being ill before she came to stay, were there? Supposing *she's* the one behind the poisoning?'

'We don't have any evidence,' Georgina reminded her. 'You know Colin's feelings about that. We can't accuse anyone without having proof.'

'I know, but it makes sense. Hugo wants to go back to London. His mum is taking his side – maybe because she's his mum, but maybe because she wants the kids living near her, so she can see more of them,' Doris said. 'And Louise wants to stay here. So maybe her mother-in-law is trying to persuade her to go back to London. And how do you persuade someone to leave? You make it hard for them to stay. If the business is shut down, Louise will lose her income and she'll have to sell up.'

'That's a motive,' Georgina said thoughtfully.

'And we know the means: minced chicken in the sausage rolls that wasn't cooked properly.'

'But how could that have happened, when Louise is so clued-up on hygiene?' Georgina asked.

'If you want something badly enough, you find a way to manage it, don't you? Hugo's mum is living with them, so she would have the opportunity to do something in the kitchen. She might even have offered to help Louise out in the bakery when she was busy,' Doris suggested. 'And of course Louise would trust her. She's the children's grandma. Like I said, flowers and serpents.' She paused. 'But what does worry me is what if she gets tired of waiting for Louise to come round to her way of thinking? What if Louise is the next one who gets poisoned? With Louise out of the way permanently, that means Hugo will be the sole parent and he can sell the mill and take the kids back to London.'

'Maybe I ought to pop round and see Louise and see if I can give her a quiet warning,' Georgina said. 'After all, we've tran-scribed Margaret's diary and I promised to keep Louise up to date. Maybe I can get her to open up a bit – and meet her mother-in-law myself.' She coughed. 'I gather she can be a bit blunt.'

'Jodie can sometimes be a little bit too sensitive,' Doris said. 'You need to make your own judgement.'

'Agreed. Will's gone into the city to have dinner with an old friend from uni who's doing a project at the Science Park,' Georgina said. 'And Colin's up to his ears and said he has no idea what time he'll be back this evening.' She glanced at her watch. 'I'll ring Louise and see if she's free now.'

Louise was not only free, she was delighted by the idea of Georgina popping round. 'You managed to transcribe the diary?'

'We did,' Georgina said. 'Unfortunately it's fairly grim reading – you can see Margaret is worried about her dad and furious with Forrest, and it builds up a picture where you can really see the miscarriage of justice about to happen.'

'But at least her voice can be heard as well as Forrest's now,' Louise said.

When Georgina went to Mill Cottage, she took Louise some flowers as well as a printout of the transcript.

Louise welcomed her warmly. The two older children were in the kitchen, dressed in pyjamas; a thin-faced woman Georgina had never met before was sitting with them, listening to the younger one read.

'Annie, this is my friend Georgina, the photographer,' Louise introduced them swiftly. 'Georgie, this is Annie, our nanny.'

'Pleased to meet you,' Georgina said with a smile, recalling that Jodie hadn't warmed to the nanny and Sam had described her as mean.

Annie simply gave her a nod of acknowledgement. Well, not everyone was chatty, and working with children didn't necessarily make you good at talking with adults, Georgina thought.

But she definitely didn't want the children to overhear some of the stuff she wanted to say to Louise, particularly as she already knew how upset Sam was. 'I was wondering, Louise,' she said. 'Could you perhaps show me where you found that diary?'

'Of course,' Louise said. 'You'll be all right with the kids for a couple of minutes, won't you, Annie?'

'Yes,' Annie agreed. She glanced at her watch. 'Isla's already asleep. Another five minutes and these two need to go to bed.'

'But I'm not tired,' Sam said. 'And I'm nine. I'm two whole years older than Noah. I want to finish reading this chapter.'

'You'll have to finish it another day. Children need their sleep,' Annie said firmly.

It was none of her business, Georgina reminded herself. And Louise was clearly happy for Annie to be in charge. Though, personally, Georgina would have let Sam stay up for another few minutes, reading.

'If you haven't already eaten, maybe you'd like to have dinner with us, Georgie,' Louise said. 'Marion's made one of her famous chilis, with her secret ingredient.'

'What, *poison*?' Doris whispered in Georgina's ear.

'Secret ingredient?' Georgina echoed.

'I think it's a couple of squares of dark chocolate, but she always shoos everyone out of the kitchen when she's cooking, so I can't say for certain,' Louise said.

Georgina really wasn't looking forward to this particular conversation, but she knew it needed to be done. 'Will your mother-in-law be joining us for dinner?' she asked.

'No.' Louise rolled her eyes. 'Would you believe, she's out at the theatre with one of her friends? She's only been living here for a couple of months, and she has a better social life than I do, what with her WI meetings, coffee mornings and trips out!'

'Or has Marion just made sure she has a cast-iron excuse not to eat the chili tonight, because she knows she's added something "special" to it?' Doris asked.

Georgina's thoughts exactly, but how could she alert Louise to the issue tactfully?

'I guess we can have a sort of girls' night in, given that Hugo had to go back to London this morning,' Louise continued.

'I'll put the chili on to reheat and put some rice on,' Annie said.

As soon as they were in the mill, out of earshot, Georgina said, 'Louise, I don't really need to see where exactly you found the diary. I'm assuming you blocked up the hole to keep the building watertight.'

'I did.' Louise looked confused. 'Why are we here then?'

'So the children can't overhear us,' Georgina said.

'That sounds serious.'

Georgina sighed. 'I apologise in advance if you think I'm interfering – it's not meant to be like that. But your Sam is good friends with the son of one of my friends, and he's worried about Sam.

Worried enough to tell his mum, who was concerned enough to ask me to help.'

Louise looked concerned. 'Why? What's Sam been saying?'

'Apparently he doesn't sleep so well on the camp bed, and I think he might have overheard a few rows between you and Hugo,' Georgina said. 'I'm not criticising. I remember what it's like having young children and a busy life, and the rows happen. But Sam's worried that you and his dad are going to get divorced and his dad will go for custody, so he, Noah and Isla will have to move back to London without you.'

Louise grimaced. 'Hugo wants us all to be back in London. But I love it here, and so do the kids. We've been making it work just fine. Well, this side of it, anyway,' she said, looking miserable. 'Hugo isn't wonderfully happy about living in a tiny flat during the week. He wants to sell the London flat and for me to sell up here, so we can buy a big Victorian terrace. Since the two food poisoning incidents, he's been on at me, saying it's a sign we ought to leave.'

'Where does your mother-in-law stand on the subject?' Georgina asked.

'Marion was supporting me, until that poor woman died – your friend, the one you said used to own Bert. Marion isn't that much younger than her, so I think maybe it spooked her.' Louise sighed. 'I don't know.'

'What do they both think about the poisonings?' Georgina asked.

'Hang on.' Louise's eyes narrowed. 'Are you saying that you think Marion was involved with it? Or Hugo?'

'It's a theory,' Georgina said. 'I don't have proof, and I've never met your mother-in-law or your husband. But I've been thinking about means and motive and opportunity. If your business goes under, it means you'll need to sell up.'

'Ye-es,' Louise said slowly.

'And if all your customers lose their faith in you – because they bought something from you, ate it and was ill, or they know someone else who was affected – that would make your business go under.'

'I really don't like where this is going,' Louise said. 'I know Marion's not on my side anymore, but I can't see her deliberately giving people food poisoning, especially children.'

'Does she miss the kids?' Georgina asked.

'Well, yes, but she knows she has a standing invite to come and stay whenever she wants,' Louise said.

'Maybe she doesn't like it here, either, and she thinks it's worth people being a little bit poorly, if that means the kids will move back to London and she gets to see them as much as she wants and stay in her own home,' Georgina said carefully. 'Or maybe she's doing it because she wants you and Hugo to stay together, instead of living apart so much of the time.'

'That makes a horrible kind of sense,' Louise said.

'This chili she cooked – did the kids have it for tea tonight?' Georgina checked.

'No. They don't like spicy food. Well, Sam does, but Annie insists on the three of them eating the same thing. She cooked them chicken tenders, mash and veg.' Louise's eyes widened. 'But Marion does make her chili with chicken mince rather than beef nowadays. She says it's healthier. Oh, my God. Are you suggesting she's behind the poisoning, and she's done something to the chili so Annie and I will be ill?'

'I don't have any evidence,' Georgina said, wincing. She could hardly tell Louise that a ghost had suggested this to her.

'Now I think about it, there was never any problem with the bakery, even when Hugo started pressuring me to sell up and move, until Marion came to stay with us after the problem with her flat,' Louise said. She blew out a breath. 'What if you're right and she *is* behind the poisoned sausage rolls? What if she's tampered with the chicken mince in the chili? She's out tonight, so she won't be there to eat it with us.'

'I think it might be a good idea to take a sample from the chili, rather than eating it,' Georgina said. 'I can get Colin to come and sort that out.'

'Thank you. And I'd better make sure Annie doesn't eat any of it – I'll have to think of something to put her off, without letting her know I suspect Marion might be trying to poison us. I'm pretty sure Annie wants to go back to London, too, so it could be that Marion's in cahoots with her. And if that's the case I don't want Marion knowing that we've rumbled her.' Louise swallowed hard. 'Then again, they might not be plotting together, because Marion doesn't particularly like our nanny. I've asked her before now if Annie's said or done something to offend her, but she just clams up and says there's something sly about the girl.' She shook her head. 'Annie's been a bit off with me, the last few weeks, even before the poisonings started. I don't know whether Marion being here has put her nose out of joint, or maybe she wanted to ask for a raise but thought I'd say no because of the problems in the business.'

'Let's use Margaret Chorley as an excuse,' Georgina said. 'We can't eat the chili yet because we're busy with the papers, and we'd very much like Annie to eat with us tonight.'

'We'll try that,' Louise decided.

Georgina texted Colin swiftly.

> Am at the Mill with Louise. Potential new suspect: Louise's mother-in-law. Can you bring some sample containers to get the chili tested? (Is made with chicken mince – like the sausage rolls...) G x

She followed up by calling Colin's mobile phone, waiting for a couple of rings and hanging up. If he hadn't spotted her text, he would see the notification for a missed call, and she knew he'd check for a message.

'Right. Now to delay that chili,' she said.

It wasn't like Georgina to call and not leave a message, Colin thought, frowning.

Then he read her text, and his frown deepened even further.

Oh, dear God. She was at the mill in Great Wenborough with a potential poisoner?

He thought back to the two previous times when Georgina had been poisoned. He'd been in time to rescue her; and admittedly this time he thought she'd be careful enough not to drink or eat anything.

But why did she think that Marion Wilkins was the poisoner? Why hadn't she shared her concerns with him so he could check it out safely, instead of being reckless and trying to sort things out by herself?

Cross that she'd taken such a risk, and worried that everything was going to go wrong, he stayed just the right side of the speed limit as he drove towards Great Wenborough. What if Georgie was right about this and Marion Wilkins was the poisoner? What if Marion realised she'd been rumbled and, thwarted of her next poisoning victim, picked up a kitchen knife instead? The potential scenarios spun through his head, worrying him even more.

True to her word, Annie had sent the boys to bed and was alone in the kitchen, doing a crossword with one eye on the stove.

'Annie, we want to do a bit of work on this diary, so we thought we'd wait a bit longer before we have dinner,' Louise said, walking into the kitchen of the mill house.

'But I've put the rice on now,' Annie said, looking put out.

'We can turn it down a bit,' Louise said. 'Or let it finish cooking and then reheat it when we're ready.'

'Reheating rice is dangerous. It's the quickest way to get food poisoning,' Annie said – and then looked horrified, as if only just remembering just how serious the food poisoning had been at the bakery, the previous week, resulting in two deaths.

'Then we can use it to make a cold rice salad for lunch tomorrow,' Louise said. 'It won't kill us to use a microwave rice pouch tonight, in that case. You don't mind waiting another half an hour before we eat, do you?'

'I wasn't going to have the chili,' Annie said. 'There's a pub quiz down at the Feathers tonight. I thought I'd go.'

Today was a Monday and Georgina was pretty sure that the regular pub quiz was on the third Thursday of the month – at least, it had been for the last couple of years. She and Colin had sometimes made up a team with Sybbie, Bernard, Francesca and Giles. Or maybe tonight was a special one-off.

'What time does it start?' Louise asked.

'Half seven,' Annie said. 'I was going to meet my friends and have a burger, first.'

Which friends? Hadn't Louise said that Annie hadn't really made friends in the village? Georgina wondered. Or maybe she was overthinking this. 'The food's good at the Feathers,' she said with a smile. 'I eat there a couple of times a month.'

Annie completely ignored Georgina. 'I'll be back about half ten, Louise,' she said. 'I'll leave you to do whatever with the rice and the chili.'

There was a faint note of contempt in her voice, Georgina thought. All of a sudden she could see exactly why Jodie didn't like the woman – and why Annie probably *hadn't* made friends locally.

Maybe she was planning to meet a boyfriend, thought Louise would disapprove, and was trying to cover her tracks. Whatever. It was none of her business. The main thing was, she and Louise weren't going to have to eat that chili.

Ten minutes after Annie had left, Colin rang the doorbell.

'There's a big difference,' he said, looking furious, 'between brainstorming ideas and doing hare-brained things like walking into a potentially dangerous situation.'

'I wasn't in any danger,' she said.

'Doris was going to protect you?' he asked, an edge to his voice.

'Who's Doris?' Louise asked.

'It's complicated,' Colin said at the same time as Georgina said,

'Pretty much my guardian angel.' And then Georgina flushed. 'It's complicated,' she muttered.

'Right.' Louise drawled the word, clearly confused. 'Can I get you some coffee, DI Bradshaw?'

'Thank you for the offer, but I'm fine,' Colin said. And his glare told Georgina that she'd better not accept a single thing to eat or drink from Louise's kitchen until he'd taken a sample of the chili and had it analysed. 'Would you care to explain the message you sent me?'

Georgina winced, and talked him through the theory of why they thought Marion Wilkins might be behind the poisoning.

'You have no evidence,' Colin said. 'It's all circumstantial.'

'But it fits. Motive, means and opportunity,' Georgina said.

'I'll take a sample and get the chili tested,' Colin said. 'I suggest you bin the rest of it, Mrs Wilkins. Georgina might be completely wrong about this.'

'And I might be right,' Georgina said, narrowing her eyes back at him.

'I think,' Louise said, 'it's going to be cheese on toast for dinner. You're both very welcome to join me.'

'That's kind,' Colin said, 'but Georgie and I need to have a talk.'

'I'll call you tomorrow,' Georgina said. 'And I'll leave the transcript for you.'

'Thank you,' Louise said. She bit her lip. 'I'm sorry if I've caused any trouble.'

'*You* haven't,' Colin said.

Georgina let him follow her back to the farmhouse. Will wasn't back yet, which was just as well because she didn't want him to overhear a fight.

'So what was that about? A dig at Doris, or a dig at me?' she demanded when they were back in her own kitchen.

'A dig at you,' he said. 'For pity's sake. That was a huge risk you took. Tackling a potential murderer.'

'Marion wasn't even there,' she pointed out.

'But she might have been.' Colin raked his hand through his hair. 'I've already sat by your hospital bedside twice. I don't want to go through that again.'

'You're not my jailer, Colin.'

'And I'm not trying to be.' He shook his head, his eyes full of anguish. 'But you were taking an unnecessary risk. You matter to me, Georgie. I don't want anything to happen to you.'

She was still annoyed enough to retort, 'I was perfectly safe.'

'Hmm,' he said. 'Well, I can't take the evidence to the lab right now. They're closed.'

'It's up to you whether you store the sample in your fridge or mine,' Georgie said coolly.

He blew out a breath. 'I don't want to fight with you, Georgie. I just worry about you.'

'Maybe you need to look at how your worry comes across,' she said. 'The words "bossy" and "control-freak" spring to mind.'

'I'm sorry. I don't mean it to be like that.' Colin crouched down to make a fuss of Bert. 'And you need a bit of peace and quiet, too. I shouldn't be shouting.'

'No, you shouldn't,' Georgina said, but this time her voice was gentler. 'Jodie dropped in, earlier. Harry's worried about Sam, who thinks his parents are going to split up and he's going to be forced to go back to London with his dad, while Louise wants to stay here.'

'It's tough on kids when their parents split up,' Colin said, clearly thinking of his own divorce.

'I just let Louise know what was going on so she can reassure him a bit,' Georgina said.

'That's kind,' Colin said. 'Well, obviously you haven't eaten. Do you want to go to the Feathers?'

'Probably not. Apparently there's a quiz night tonight. Annie – the nanny – was going,' Georgina said.

Colin frowned. 'Are you sure? It's not the third Thursday of the month.'

'I know.' Georgina shrugged. 'Maybe it's a one-off.'

'Maybe. Chinese takeaway, then?' he suggested. 'Delivered to the door?'

'That'd be good,' she said.

The next morning, Georgina and Colin were eating breakfast in the kitchen when his work phone rang.

'Yes. Right. I'm on my way.' He ended the call and looked at Georgina. 'I've been called out to Great Wenborough Mill.'

'What's happened?' Georgina asked.

'There's been an unexpected death,' he said grimly.

Georgina stared at him. 'Who?'

'That's the problem,' Colin said. 'It's Marion Wilkins.'

THIRTEEN

Georgina stared at Colin, her face white with shock. 'What? Marion Wilkins is dead? But... she was the one I thought was the poisoner. The one who had a motivation, the means and an opportunity.'

'Clearly someone else had all of that, too,' Colin said.

'Oh, my God.' She shook her head, obviously trying to clear it. 'I ought to ring Louise.'

'Leave it for a little while,' Colin said, trying hard not to sound bossy; at the same time, this was his investigation, and he needed Georgina to give him the space to do his job. 'I need to interview Louise and everyone else in the house, first, to piece together what happened last night. I'll call you when I'm done.'

'All right.' She gave him a rueful smile. 'Don't forget the chili sample you took last night is still in my fridge.'

'Can I get it picked up later, so I can send it in with the other samples being taken this morning?' Colin asked, not wanting to take her for granted.

'Of course. Anything you need, just let me know.' She looked at him. 'Don't eat or drink anything at the mill, no matter what they offer you.'

He coughed. 'What was that you were saying yesterday about "bossy" and "control-freak"?'

'All right, all right,' she said crossly. 'You had a valid point. I worry about you, too.'

'I know.' He kissed her lightly. 'I'd better go. I'll keep you posted.'

Larissa and Mo were already there when he got to the mill.

'Mrs Wilkins, I'm very sorry for your loss,' Colin said to Louise, who was sitting at the kitchen table. 'Would you mind answering a few questions for me?'

'I – of course. I can't believe...' She looked and sounded dazed. 'Marion was always so *alive*.'

Past tense, he thought. 'Take me through what happened last night,' he said gently. 'Is there somewhere quiet we can sit?'

'Uh – the ground floor of the mill?' she suggested.

'That's fine,' he said. Once she'd unlocked the door and they were both settled, he said, 'When you're ready, tell me what happened in your own words.'

'Marion was out at the theatre, last night – she'd gone with friends she met through the WI. She always loved a show, and it was a comedian she'd seen on the telly and liked,' Louise said. 'As you know, she made us a chili for dinner last night – the chili we thought she might have laced with something, which is why you took a sample. She couldn't have eaten any before she left, because if she was the poisoner, she'd know not to touch it, and besides she seemed absolutely fine when she left here.'

'And that was roughly what time?' Colin asked.

'Her friend Babs picked her up about half past six. They were going to park near to the theatre and have a drink in the bar. She said she thought she'd be home by about half past ten.'

'Is that when she got home?' Colin asked.

'I'm really not sure,' Louise said. 'I had an early night. I had some cheese on toast – that must have been about half past seven – and then I realised how tired I was. Obviously, with everything that's been going on around here, I haven't been sleeping well.

With the children asleep and the house quiet, I decided to have an early night. I went to bed and started reading the transcript of the diary Georgina printed out for me. I must have fallen asleep in the middle of it, because I woke up this morning and the papers were all over the place.'

'Was anyone else in the house with you?'

'The children, obviously,' Louise said. 'Our nanny – Annie Newman – is usually here, but she went out last night, too. A pub quiz, she said.'

The pub quiz that Colin didn't think existed. Who had Annie Newman met instead? he wondered. 'What time did she go out?'

'About ten minutes before you got here, yesterday evening,' Louise said. 'I don't know what time she got back. I must have been asleep. I didn't hear her come in.'

'She has a key to the front door?'

'Of course,' Louise said.

'Do you have a security doorbell?' Colin asked.

'Yes, but it doesn't record at night. Hugo got fed up of being woken up every time a fox went through the garden or a bat flew past and set a notification off on my phone.' She gave him a wan smile. 'I didn't think to turn it back on when he's not here.'

So there wouldn't be any timestamped footage of when Annie and Marion had returned to the house, then. 'OK,' he said. 'What happened this morning?'

'Marion's staying with us at the moment while her flat's being sorted – she had a leak, and while the builders were fixing it, they found asbestos in the ceiling. Obviously she's had to move out until it's sorted. She's got a bad knee so she can't manage the stairs, so Hugo moved the furniture round in the dining room to make it into a proper bedroom, and he brought Sam's bed down for her – Sam's sleeping on a camp bed,' Louise explained. 'I was up early. I'm usually in the bakery kitchen for half past four to do the prep on the sourdough, so I'm done in time to get the kids up at quarter to seven. Annie was checking they had their stuff for school and nursery while they ate their breakfast. I made Marion a cup of tea at about quarter to eight, and I thought it was a bit strange that she didn't answer when I knocked. She's normally awake well before then. I suppose I assumed she was sleeping in after a late night. I opened the door, and that was when I realised there was a horrible smell in the room.'

Death, vomit and faeces. Which was a shock to the system even when you'd come across it a few times, Colin thought. 'Take your time, Mrs Wilkins,' he said gently.

'She was just lying there on the floor, not even in bed. Face down on the floorboards. I grabbed my phone to ring for an ambulance. I went over to see if I could find a pulse while I was waiting for them to answer, but she was cold to the touch. She must have died hours ago. I closed the door behind me and went out into the garden so the children couldn't hear me talking to the emergency services, and when I'd finished I told Annie she needed to get the children up and out of the house quickly, to school. I turned my back so the children couldn't see my face, and mouthed to her that Marion was dead. She took the children to school, and then the paramedics turned up with your colleagues.'

'Sammy Granger, the pathologist, will be here shortly, too,' he said. 'We need to establish whether Marion died from natural causes.'

'She was sick. Maybe she choked on her own vomit. Maybe she'd gone down with some sort of bug.' Louise's eyes were filled with tears. 'What a horrible way to go. I know we'd had a bit of a falling-out over the last couple of weeks, but until then we'd always managed to rub along well enough. She's a bit quick to speak her mind and she doesn't always think about people's feelings before she opens her mouth and says something, but I suppose her generation is a bit prone to that.' She swallowed hard. 'The children are going to be devastated. And I don't know how I'm going to tell Hugo that he's lost his mum.'

'You haven't told him yet?'

'I haven't been able to get hold of him,' Louise confirmed. 'He's always in the office early, but he keeps his personal phone on silent. He won't have picked up my message to call me urgently, but even if he had, he might not have had the time yet. He's a hedge fund manager,' she explained. 'Before the markets open, he looks at the global news, market data and broker reports, to see if anything's likely to affect his investments, and then he's busy monitoring everything when the markets open, and then there's the research and financial models to sort out when the markets close.'

'I can contact my colleagues and ask them to send someone to break the news to him for you,' he said.

'Thank you. He needs to know, and I...' Her voice tailed off. 'What happens now?' she asked. 'Do you have to investigate Marion's death?'

'If she hasn't seen a doctor in the past few weeks and her death wasn't expected, then we'll need to notify the coroner,' he said gently. 'We need to establish the cause of Marion's death, and that's one of the reasons I'm asking you questions now, to help establish the circumstances around her death. Sometimes it means the funeral will have to be delayed, but I promise you we'll treat her with respect and dignity and do our best to help you.'

'I just can't believe I won't ever see her again,' Louise said. 'None of this seems real.'

Her shock and grief seemed genuine, Colin thought. 'Is there anything else you can think of that happened?' he asked.

'Nothing,' she said. 'I'm sorry. It's all a blur.'

'OK. And remember I asked you to dispose of the chili – what did you do with it?' he asked.

Louise's face lost all its colour. 'Oh, my God. I was so thrown by everything that happened, I didn't put it in the bin – I left it in the saucepan, on top of the hob. Could she have heated up a bowl of it in the microwave?'

'It's a possibility,' Colin acknowledged.

'So *I* killed her,' Louise said, her eyes wide with horror.

'Let's wait to see what the pathologist says,' Colin suggested. 'When will Miss Newman be back?'

'About nine. She drops Sam and Noah at the middle school, then Isla at the kindergarten,' Louise said.

'All right. I'll write up what you've told me, and ask you to check your statement and sign it,' Colin said.

By the time that was all sorted, Annie Newman was back at the cottage.

'Could you take me through events of last night, in your own words?' he asked.

'I went to the Feathers with my friends,' she said, but he noticed that she didn't meet his eye.

'I'll need their names and addresses,' he said.

'I don't know where they live. Just their names,' she said quickly. 'Tom. He's one of them. And Spike.'

Names Colin knew; Tom Nichols, known as 'Young Tom', had a gardening business and happened to be Georgina's gardener; and his grandfather, known as 'Old Tom', was Sybbie's head gardener at the Manor. Spike, Tom's best friend, was a mechanic who played guitar in a local band. 'Do you have their phone numbers?' he asked.

'I don't know them that well,' she said. 'I just... hang about with the group in the Feathers.'

'How did you know when and where to meet them last night if you don't have their phone numbers and they don't have yours?' he asked.

Annie's cheeks pinkened. 'They mentioned it last time I saw them,' she said.

It sounded as if Tom had tried to be kind, with a casual 'see you here the same time next week' sort of suggestion, Colin thought. 'How long were you there?' he asked.

'From about seven until quarter past ten. Then I walked back here.'

'Was Mrs Wilkins – Marion,' he clarified, 'home by then?'

'I have no idea,' Annie said. 'I just cleaned my teeth and went to bed.'

'Did you hear anyone come in after you?'

'No. She sleeps downstairs, so I wouldn't have heard the stairs creaking,' she said. 'I didn't hear anything. I must have just fallen asleep.'

'And Mrs Wilkins – Louise – wasn't still up when you came home?'

'No. I think her bedside light might have still been on – you can see the light through the gap at the bottom of the door – but I didn't speak to her.'

'OK,' Colin said. 'Talk me through this morning.'

'I got up, had a shower and got dressed. I got the baby dressed, told the boys to hurry up, then sorted their schoolbags out. I normally do that the night before, but I forgot last night because I was looking forward to seeing my friends,' Annie said. 'They'd had their breakfast and I was just nagging them to do their teeth when Louise made a cup of tea for Mrs Wilkins. Then I heard the front door close, so I assume she'd popped out for some milk or something. When she came back in, she made sure the kids couldn't see her face and told me Mrs Wilkins was dead, and I needed to get the kids out of the house before the ambulance got here. Louise didn't want Sam to worry because he's had a bit of a tricky time lately and we've had to do a bit of extra washing,' she said.

'Got you,' Colin said. This wasn't the first case he'd worked on where a vulnerable young boy had been distressed to the point of wetting the bed.

'So that's what I did. I took the kids to school, and when I got back here you lot were all here.'

Again, Colin wrote up the statement and asked her to read it through, correct it where necessary and sign it.

By that time, Sammy Granger, the pathologist, had arrived.

'Ballpark? I'd say the time of death was between about midnight and one in the morning,' she said when Colin asked for her opinion. 'It could be natural causes. But I'd say it's much more likely that she choked on her own vomit. Something made her sick. Do you know if she was a habitual drinker?'

'I'll check,' Colin said. Even now, after years of being sober, he felt a hot flush of shame when someone casually mentioned alcohol being a potential cause of death. 'Could campylobacter poisoning have made her sick?'

'Diarrhoea is more common with campylobacter than vomiting,' Sammy said. 'It would be watery, blood-stained, and usually goes together with painful stomach cramps. Is this linked to the campylobacter outbreak from last week?'

'Possibly,' he said. 'I also need to know what Marion's last meal was. Did she eat chili last night?'

They'd been here before, in a case involving a poisoned curry, and Sammy had been extremely helpful. 'I'll let you know. Is there any particular poison you want me to look out for?' she asked.

'The one that killed Miss Hurst,' he said.

'Rat poison. Specifically, brodifacoum. Got you,' she said.

'I've also got a sample of the chili in Georgie's fridge,' he said. 'That might be helpful.'

'Why did you take a sample last night?' she asked.

He winced. 'Georgie had a hunch that the chili might have been poisoned.'

'The same chili this poor woman ate?'

'It's a possibility,' Colin said.

'If her last meal was poisoned chili, then a sample untouched by gastric fluids would be very useful,' Sammy said.

'Marion Wilkins was the one who made the chili,' Colin said.

Sammy frowned. 'If she made the chili and added poison to it, then why would she eat it? And who was she planning to poison?'

'I don't know why she ate it, but Louise was the potential victim,' Colin said quietly. 'Possibly the nanny, too. And maybe Georgie as well, though she wouldn't have known Georgie was coming round.'

'Why?' Sammy asked.

'That,' Colin said, 'is one of the things I want to find out.' Was Marion still a suspect, or was she simply a victim? And if she wasn't the one to poison the chili, that left Louise and Annie as potential suspects.

He needed to get that chili tested. Fast.

Just after lunch, someone leaned on Georgina's doorbell.

'I'll get it, Mum,' Will said. He came back a few seconds later, ushering Louise into the kitchen. Her face was wet with tears and she was struggling to breathe. 'Deep breaths, in for four and out for four,' he said. 'I'll count for you.'

It took ten rounds of him being very calm and patient, but eventually Louise was breathing normally again, and Georgina handed her a glass of water.

'Are the children all right? What's happened?' she asked.

'Babs phoned – the woman from the WI that Marion was friendly with. She couldn't get an answer from Marion's mobile, so she rang the house landline.' Louise was shaking. 'I had to tell her Marion was dead, and the police are investigating. She said Marion was absolutely fine when she dropped Marion back here last night. And then...' She closed her eyes. 'Oh, God. She told me Marion confided in her, a couple of days ago. Somehow she found out that Hugo was having an affair.' She dragged in a breath. 'She talked to Babs about it again last night, and Babs urged her to tell me what she knew. Except I was asleep by the time she came home, and she never got the chance to discuss it with me.'

'I'm so sorry,' Georgina said. On top of dealing with her business running into trouble, her husband being unsupportive and wanting her to sell up, and the death of her mother-in-law, now Louise had to deal with her husband having an affair. 'Did she know who he was seeing?'

Louise nodded. 'Annie.'

'The nanny?' Will asked.

'Yes. I'm so angry, I could kill both of them myself,' Louise said. 'Obviously I won't actually kill them, but...' Her face tightened. 'I want both of them out of the house.'

'Before you do anything,' Georgina counselled, 'I think you should talk to Colin.' And she felt incredibly guilty, because she'd jumped to conclusions and assumed that Marion was the one with the motive. Now, it looked more as if the poisoner was someone else. If Annie knew that Marion had found out about the affair and was planning to tell Louise, then maybe *she'd* been the one to poison the chili. Marion would eat it and die before telling Louise; Louise would also die, leaving Hugo free to make his affair with Annie a more official relationship – and which, horribly, echoed the rumours Herbert Forrest had started about Margaret Chorley. Annie, going to the quiz night and planning a burger with her friends, had an alibi and could say that she, too, thought Marion was behind the poisonings. And Georgina herself would have been collateral damage.

Dead.

She picked up her phone and speed-dialled Colin.

'I'm really sorry, Georgie, but I can't talk now,' Colin said when he answered.

'I don't want to talk to you,' Georgina said. 'I want you to talk to Louise. Because there's been a development and you have a new suspect with a completely different motive...'

FOURTEEN

Colin listened to Louise's statement coolly and calmly.

That definitely changed things.

Depending on whether or not Marion Wilkins had eaten some of the chili, it was looking as if Marion was the victim rather than the poisoner. And he needed to interview Annie Newman again.

'Annie definitely doesn't know that you know about her affair with your husband?' he checked.

'I didn't know anything until Babs told me, and Annie was out when Babs rang,' Louise confirmed.

'Good. Do you know where Annie is at the moment?' he asked.

'She said she was going to do some shopping, then call into the supermarket to get something for the children's tea on her way to pick them up from school,' Louise said.

'Would you be able to pick them up, instead?' Colin asked. 'Because I need a chat with her.'

'I'll be there,' Louise said.

'Thank you,' Colin said. He asked her for Babs's full name and number – which Louise didn't have, but said she could get from the landline phone's memory and send to him when she was home again – and the details of the car Annie was driving. Then he asked, 'Would you mind passing me back to Georgina, please?'

'Of course,' Louise said.

'Georgie, I need to interview Annie Newman. I'm planning to intercept her before she picks the children up, but I don't want her to see Louise or her car in case it tips her off that something's not quite right. Would you be able to take Louise to the school?' Colin asked.

'Better than that. I'll ask her to ring the school with permission for Jodie pick them up,' Georgina said. 'Then she can collect them from Jodie, or Jodie can bring them here.'

'So Annie won't see Louise at all. That's perfect,' Colin said. 'Thank you. And if you could take Louise back to the mill to get Babs's number, that would be brilliant.'

'No problem. Keep me posted,' she said.

'Will do,' he promised.

His next call was to Sammy Granger. 'Sorry to ask,' he said, 'but I have a new development. Have you had a chance to do the PM on Marion Wilkins yet?'

'I have – and you were right,' Sammy said. 'Her last meal was eaten no more than a couple of hours before she died; it was chili, and it was laced with rat poison. The samples you sent were of the same chili. That was laced with rat poison, too.'

'The same type as the one that killed Miss Hurst?' Colin checked.

'Exactly the same,' Sammy confirmed. 'Brodifacoum.'

'Thank you,' Colin said.

When he ended the call, he had a quick briefing meeting with Mo and Larissa, his sergeant and his constable, to bring them up to speed with the new information. He asked Mo to get the permissions to look into Annie Newman's financial records and Larissa to join him in arresting Annie just before school pickup. Georgina had sent him Barbara Kelly's contact details, and Colin had a very illuminating conversation with her confirming everything Louise had told him.

Colin and Larissa were waiting outside the school when Annie Newman parked her car.

'Annie Newman, I'm arresting you on suspicion of the murder of Marion Wilkins last night,' Colin said. 'We have evidence that shows you may have been involved, and your arrest is necessary to question you about your involvement.'

Larissa followed with the official caution.

'You have the right to representation,' Colin continued. 'We can call the duty solicitor for you, or you can call your own legal counsel if you prefer.'

Annie stared at them, and he saw her expression change from defiance to defeat as she clearly worked out that he already knew most of what had happened.

'The duty solicitor will do,' she said.

Ignoring the interested looks of the mums gathering outside the school gates, Colin and Larissa walked her to the car and took her into Norwich.

Back at the station, Larissa organised a hot drink and something to eat for Annie as they waited for the duty solicitor to arrive. After the duty solicitor had had a few minutes alone in the interview room with Annie, Colin and Larissa joined them. Colin set the tape running, stated the names of everyone present and the time, and repeated the caution. Hopefully Mo would come up with something in the financials to prove what Colin already suspected.

'When we spoke earlier today,' Colin said quietly, 'you held some information back. You didn't get on well with Marion Wilkins, did you?'

'I didn't have much to do with her. Louise employs me to look after the children,' Annie said.

He noted that she referred to Louise as her employer, rather than Louise and Hugo.

'That doesn't quite answer my question. You didn't get on with Marion, did you?'

'She was nosey,' Annie muttered. 'And she thought she could say whatever she liked.'

'What did she say to upset you, Annie?' Larissa asked.

'She was always going on about how I should know my place –
as if I was some kind of servant,' Annie said, lifting her chin. 'She
was rude to me.'

'Or was it more that she was trying to protect her son's
marriage?' Colin asked quietly.

The colour drained from Annie's face. 'I don't know what you
mean.'

'You were having an affair with Hugo Wilkins,' Colin said.

'I...' Annie looked miserable, and nodded.

'How did she find out?' Larissa asked.

'She saw us together in the kitchen. We weren't doing
anything,' Annie added hastily. 'He'd been about to kiss me, but he
hadn't. Maybe she thought we were standing a bit too close
together or something. He told me later that day we had to cool
things between us until his mother went back to London.'

'When was this?' Colin asked.

'Before Christmas,' Annie said. 'And I could feel her watching
me. All the time.'

'Did she threaten to tell Louise?' Larissa asked.

'She didn't put it like that.'

'How did she put it?' Colin asked.

'She kept saying that it might be an idea for me to move on –
that a girl like me couldn't be happy stuck in a backwater like
Great Wenborough.'

'Was she right? Were you unhappy here?' Larissa asked, her
voice kind.

'Nothing ever happens in Great Wenborough!' Annie burst
out. 'All the school mums look down on me because I'm a nanny,
not one of them. They do things together – cliquey things like
going out for coffee and Pilates classes, and they have girly nights
out. They ask Louise, who never goes because she's always too
busy with her bloody mill and the bakery, but they never ask *me*.
The ones at the nursery are all wrapped up in their babies and
can't talk about anything else. There's nowhere to go in the evening
except the pub, and have you ever tried walking into a pub on your

own where everyone stares at you because you didn't grow up round here and you're not one of them?'

Annie had clearly been lonely and bored and isolated. Had Hugo seen that, and realised she would be easy prey for him? Colin wondered. Had he promised Annie things he had no intention of doing? Colin had a list of questions he wanted to put to Hugo Wilkins; given that Hugo was in London, and might not have rushed back to his family even once he knew of his mother's death, Colin knew exactly who wanted to ask those questions for him. Inspector Mei Zhang would get straight to the point – and she'd make sure she got an answer.

'When did the affair start?' Colin asked.

'In the summer holidays,' Annie admitted.

'Who started it?' Colin asked, keeping his voice deliberately non-judgemental.

'I saw him looking at me,' Annie said. 'You know the sort of look. When you fancy someone and you know you shouldn't do anything about it, but you can't help yourself. And he must have seen me looking at him, the same way. I knew he wasn't doing it with Louise – she was always working – and a man has needs, you know?'

Colin thought of Georgina. 'Yeah. I know,' he said gruffly.

'I'd got a day off. Louise had taken the kids to the beach for a picnic. Hugo was working from home. I took him a cup of coffee. He looked pleased and said he could kiss me for that. And I said he could, if he wanted. He closed his laptop and we... we did it on the dining room table. And wherever else, when we got the chance.' Once she'd confession, the words flowed. Hugo had told her he'd had enough of Norfolk, but Louise was being stubborn. Him staying in London for weekdays wasn't enough to pressure her into selling up and moving. If he could find a way of getting the family back to London, then he'd set Annie up in a flat and they could be together more easily. Then, once the mill was sold, he'd have the funds to divorce Louise and they could be together.

'But then his mum moved in and it ruined everything. She

found out about us. I don't know how. I was discreet,' Annie said. 'Hugo knew I'd wait for him. He told me we had to cool it a bit, just until his mum's flat was fixed. But I knew she was going to tell Louise, and that would ruin everything.'

'So you decided to get rid of her,' Larissa said.

'I... I was getting wound up by her. Me and Hugo, we hadn't managed to be together for ages. Only phone calls, where we pretended...' She flushed, and broke off.

At that point, Mo interrupted, asking for a brief word with Colin. Although his expression was neutral, the fact he'd interrupted an interview told Colin this would be significant information.

Colin stopped the tape. 'Five minutes comfort break,' he said, and left the room with Mo.

'Online payment,' Mo said, and gave Colin a printout.

Colin looked at it. 'If she'd bought the rat poison in a shop for cash, we would have had more of a problem linking her to it.'

'Interviews and CCTV, depending on whether it was a little corner shop or a massive DIY warehouse,' Mo said. 'It would have taken a bit longer, yes, but we would have got the result in the end.'

'Nice work,' Colin said. 'I need you to talk to Mei Zhang and ask her to question Hugo Wilkins for me under caution.' He filled Mo in on what Annie had told him. 'I need to know if the poisoning was solely Annie's idea, or if it was his and he groomed her, or if they came up with it together.'

Back in the interview room, he started the tape and did the usual admin before launching back into questioning. 'Where were we? Marion Wilkins. She was getting in your way. You decided to take her out. But you weren't entirely sure it would work or how much poison you'd need to make an adult ill, or whether the spices would be enough to disguise the taste of the poison, so you did a test run. You knew Louise liked the chili-chicken sausage rolls. And you knew her children didn't like spicy food, so you thought the kids in Sam's class probably wouldn't touch them either and you'd be safe just adding a bit of rat poison to the sausage rolls only

Louise would eat. But you'd cover it up by putting something in the plain ones that would make the kids ill. Nobody would think there might be two different poisons involved, if all the children and their teacher went down with food poisoning.'

'That's not true. I didn't do anything to make the kids ill,' Annie said. 'I wouldn't ever hurt kids.'

But she didn't deny trying to poison Louise's spicy sausage rolls, Colin thought. Time to push a bit harder – and if he ignored what she'd said, maybe that would push her into admitting something. 'And you remembered what Hugo said about finding a way to force Louise to sell up and go back to London. Maybe the poison could help with that, too. All the kids being ill would throw suspicion on Louise's business. Dosing a second batch to affect a wider customer base after the health and safety team cleared the bakery was a masterstroke. The whole village was talking – Little Wenborough, too – and Louise had to close her doors for a second investigation. You knew Billy the butcher would be all right, because he comes from round here and his family has run the village butchery for decades, so everyone would be sure he wasn't the one behind the poison. Louise is an outsider, so people would suspect her. Her customers would forgive the first lot because anyone can make a mistake, but a second lot of poisoning would clearly mean it was deliberate rather than an accident and she couldn't be trusted. If she's even allowed to reopen the bakery, her customers might not want to come back. Then Louise would have no choice: she'd have to sell and go back to London – and you could be with Hugo.'

Annie shook her head. 'It wasn't like that.'

'Then how was it, Annie?' Colin asked gently. 'Tell me.'

Annie clammed up again.

OK. He'd have to go back to his original thesis, then. 'But Marion was there, ready to put a spoke in your wheel by telling Louise what you'd done with Hugo. Then all your hard work to ruin the business would have been for nothing. So you decided to get rid of her,' Colin continued. 'And then you realised you could get rid of Louise, at the same time. Marion was so proud of her chili and its special secret ingredient. You waited until she'd made a batch – you might even have suggested she should make it, to cheer Louise up. And then you added your own secret ingredient. The rat poison. Which you bought online, and we have the electronic trail to prove it.' Colin paused. 'You normally eat with the family, but last night you went to the pub instead.'

'For the quiz night,' Annie said.

'The Feathers happens to be my local,' Colin said mildly. 'Quiz night is the third Thursday of the month. Which wasn't last night. So who were you really meeting? Hugo?'

'No! I went to the pub! I told you, I was with Young Tom and Spike and that lot,' Annie protested.

'Whose quiz team is called the Young Ones. It's a play on Tom's nickname, plus his granddad is a huge Rik Mayall fan and brought Tom up on the same kind of comedy,' Colin said. 'I spoke to Young Tom earlier. He knows who you are, but he says you're not one of his circle of friends.'

Tears welled in Annie's eyes, though he wasn't sure whether they were from anger, frustration or misery. 'It's so unfair. They just won't let you in unless you're born round here.'

That wasn't strictly true – he and Georgina had been welcomed by the community – but Colin decided not to make Annie feel worse on that front. He wanted her to tell him the truth, and bullying her wouldn't help her do that. 'Fortunately for you, Sally, the landlady, said you were there all evening.' On her own. 'But your plan to get rid of Louise didn't quite work. She didn't eat the chili.' Thanks to Georgie's warning. 'But Marion did. And she's dead. That's the third person you've killed: Miss Hurst, Valerie Waring, and Marion Wilkins. Not to mention all the people you've made ill – and Bert.'

'What? Who's Valerie Waring? And who's Bert?' Annie demanded.

Colin wondered if Annie realised what she'd just admitted. Not that it mattered. 'Valerie is a local member of the community who died from campylobacter, and Bert is my partner's dog. I carried him into the vet's, the morning after he ate the sausage rolls you'd infected with campylobacter.' And he never wanted to see that kind of devastation in Georgina's face again.

'But I don't know anything about campylobacter,' Annie said. 'That wasn't me. I'd never hurt a dog. Why would you think I'd do that?'

'But the other two deaths were because of you,' Larissa said.

'No,' Annie protested.

'The pathology results are the same for both Miss Hurst and Marion Wilkins. We know the same rat poison was used – brodifacoum. We also have the details of your online purchase of rat poison,' Colin said. 'Which happens to be brodifacoum.'

Annie stared at him, blanching.

'It's not the same poison that Riley uses for his customers – that's in grain that's been dyed blue, and it would be visible in food.' Just as Will had told him that the Arsenic Act of 1851 had insisted that arsenic had to be coloured by soot or indigo so it couldn't be 'accidentally' added to food. 'You bought red blocks, and once you'd grated it up, the shavings would look like chili flakes so they'd be easy to hide in the spicy sausage rolls and the chili.'

Her shoulders sagged. 'I didn't think it would actually *kill* someone.'

'Didn't you?' he enquired coolly. 'Surely it's obvious that rat poison would cause actually bodily harm, and potentially death.'

'But I didn't put that much in the sausage rolls or the chili!' Annie protested. 'And humans are so much bigger than rats. There wasn't enough to kill anyone.'

'Surely Miss Hurst's death would have made you realise that putting a small amount of rat poison in the chili would kill whoever ate it?' Larissa asked. 'And Louise had a guest, last night. You could have killed Georgina Drake.'

'I wasn't expecting her to turn up,' Annie said. Her expression turned sulky. 'Anyway, she was poking around in things that weren't her business.'

'She was looking into the cold case of a miller's daughter who was falsely accused of poisoning someone,' Colin said. 'Whereas you've poisoned countless people and tried to pin it on Louise.'

'No, I haven't!' Annie insisted. 'I had nothing to do with the campylobacter.'

'Then who did?' Larissa asked.

Annie shook her head. 'I don't know.'

'I think you're lying,' Larissa said, 'to try and make your crimes look less serious. You killed two people in cold blood with the rat poison, and would have killed more if Louisa and Georgina had eaten that chili. And you interfered with the other sausage rolls so the campylobacter would make everything more complicated. All those people you made ill.' She folded her arms. 'Including one of the children you're supposed to be looking after.'

'I didn't! I would never have hurt Sam.'

It didn't quite add up, Colin thought. Annie had admitted more or less to the rat poison, and they had the evidence to back that up. But the campylobacter really did make everything more complicated. Either Annie had worked with the suspect he had in mind, or she was protecting that person. Georgina had originally thought that Marion was behind the campylobacter; but Colin was hoping that Mei's questioning in London would prove that his new suspect was the guilty party.

'I'll need to keep you in custody, Annie,' he said, 'until the Crown Prosecution Service decide to charge you formally in front of a magistrate.'

FIFTEEN

'I think we have two poisoners,' he said to Mo and Larissa. 'The question is whether Hugo Wilkins was working in league with Annie, or whether he planned to let her take the blame for all of it. I've told Mei my theories, so hopefully she'll find out the truth for us.' He drummed his fingers on his desk in frustration. 'I'd rather be the one interviewing Hugo Wilkins, but I can't justify haring off to London – not when we have colleagues on the spot who can do the job for us and we have enough to do here.'

'Mei's good, guv,' Mo reminded him. 'She'll get to the bottom of it.'

'I know,' Colin agreed. 'Though it's frustrating not to tie up all the loose ends myself.'

A few minutes later, Mei rang. 'You were right,' she said. 'Hugo denied it at first, and did a lot of blustering about why were we wasting time on him when we should be finding out who killed his mother. But then I told him we knew about his affair with Annie. I suggested he might have groomed her. Then he crumpled and told us what we wanted to know.'

'Let me put you on speaker in the breakout room,' Colin said, and ushered Mo and Larissa into the quiet room off the open-plan office. 'We're all ears.'

'Thanks to you telling us Annie's version of events, I was able to push him quite hard. He admitted he started the affair, and he knew he shouldn't have done it – she's twenty years younger than he is, she works for his family and he had a duty of care towards her. But he was miserable in Norfolk, so was she, and according to him they merely grabbed a bit of happiness together while they could.' She sighed. 'I hate that kind of self-justification. He even said, "Boys will be boys."'

'Oh, that's vile. Did he do the smirk when he said it?' Larissa asked.

'Yes,' Mei said. 'How anyone could think an attitude like that is valid in this day and age is beyond me. Apart from the fact that a man in his forties most definitely doesn't count as a boy, that kind of entitled, selfish behaviour isn't acceptable among young males, either. Anyway. He wanted to move back to London full-time, but the only way he could afford it was if they sold the Norfolk property. Apparently his big, fat bonuses haven't been big or fat the last few years, and I get the impression his job might be hanging from a thread. Annie might have thought she was going to get a man with a flashy job who could keep her in luxury, but I think she would have got a disappointment.'

'Did he groom Annie to do the poisoning?' Colin asked.

'Actually, no. He did that all himself,' Mei reported. 'He knew the school trip was coming up. He said he'd stay a bit longer at the weekend to help. Meanwhile, he put the dead rat in the grain store, knowing the kids would see it and report it back to their parents. One of his mates at work had been ill over Christmas with food poisoning – apparently it happens a lot because people don't cool the turkey properly before they put it in the fridge – and it gave him the idea of doctoring the sausage rolls. He read online about campylobacter; all he had to do was get a bit of the raw minced chicken Louise used in the sausage rolls, leave it out of the fridge for a few hours so it'd go off, and then mix it in with the rest of the mince, because cooking the sausage rolls wouldn't be quite enough to kill off all the bacteria. He put it in a storage container hidden in his gym bag, so if Louise noticed any smell she would assume it was his gym trainers and wouldn't investigate.'

'That's *so* gross,' Mo said, pulling a face.

'Isn't it?' Mei said, sounding disgusted.

'That school trip included his own son,' Colin said. 'I can't understand why anyone would deliberately make their own child ill.'

'It didn't even occur to him that his son would be affected,' Mei said. 'He was completely fixated on a means to an end. His plan worked. The children all fell ill, Louise's business was investigated by the health and safety team and people in the village gossiped about the situation. He came home from London early on the pretext of being supportive – and then tampered with the chicken a second time, to make sure this time the business would be shut down and people would be really suspicious of her.'

'Why didn't Louise notice that the chicken smelled a bit funny?' Mo asked.

'I'm guessing she was distracted with worry,' Mei said. 'Hugo said something about chopped fresh herbs. It probably helped to mask the scent. And Louise didn't know to look out for someone tampering with her food.'

'What was Annie's role in all this?' Colin asked.

'I thought he was going to try pinning the blame on her – but instead he said that he never intended to get together with her when they were back in London. He was getting bored with her and he'd been trying to distance himself from her. Then he admitted that his mum had guessed what was going on and gave him an ultimatum: break it off, or she'd tell Louise about his affair with the nanny.'

'Did he tell Annie to put poison in the chili?' Colin asked.

'I don't think so. He was shocked when I told him the cause of his mother's death. And then he said if he found out who did it, he'd kill them.'

'Considering he'd already killed Valerie Waring and made a lot of other people ill, as well as Bert – Georgina's dog – that's a bit rich,' Colin said.

'He doesn't know it was Annie who killed his mum. I've left him in custody for the time being,' Mei said, 'but I'm pretty sure the Crown Prosecution Service will charge him with manslaughter, at the very least.'

'I'd go for murder. Valerie was fragile to start with. Push the eggshell skull rule,' Colin advised.

'It's going to be tricky for you, having to tell Louise Wilkins that her nanny murdered an innocent teacher and Louise's mother-in-law, and planned to bump her off and take her place. Or that her husband was the one behind the plot to ruin her business, and killed someone in the process,' Mei said.

'Or that he didn't care if their own son became seriously ill, either. It's a mess,' Colin agreed. 'I don't think she'll stand by either of them. And I don't blame her. In her shoes, I wouldn't, either.'

Before he and Larissa went to see Louise, he called in to Rookery Farm.

'Was Marion killed by rat poison?' Georgina asked.

'Yes,' he said, 'though I didn't come to tell you about that. I know who doctored the sausage rolls that killed Valerie and nearly did for Bert. Although normally I shouldn't—'

'—be discussing a case, I know,' she cut in, 'but this is personal.'

He nodded. 'And it involves Bert, which is why I'm telling you. It was Hugo. He mixed chicken mince that had gone off with the fresh chicken mince.'

'So that's where the campylobacter came from,' she said. 'But surely after the first bite people would have realised that the sausage roll didn't taste right? And I know spaniels are greedy, but Bert never eats any rotten stuff he finds when we're out on a walk.'

'There were herbs in the mixture,' he reminded her. 'Maybe there were just enough to disguise the taste.'

She frowned. 'But I don't understand why Hugo would do something like that in the first place.'

'He thought if Louise's business went under, she'd be forced to agree to go back to London,' Colin explained.

Her frown deepened. 'Didn't he think about the people he'd be making ill? For pity's sake – it was his own son's class on that school trip. Valerie *died*, and Bert was seriously ill.'

'Clearly he didn't think it through,' Colin said. 'But he'll face the courts. I think he'll be on a charge for manslaughter for Valerie. He'll also be charged with causing unnecessary suffering to Bert. I'll be recommending the most severe sentence for what he did.'

'I'd like to break every bone in his body,' Georgina said, looking fiercer than he'd ever seen her. '*Twice*. And then carve out his heart – or whatever shrivelled husk passes for it – with a rusty spoon,' she added, her voice harsh.

'A rusty spoon isn't sharp,' Colin pointed out.

'Precisely,' Georgina said.

He gave her a hug. 'I know where you're coming from, and I probably shouldn't say it but I'm with you. But,' he added, 'vigilante justice isn't real justice. Trust the courts. He'll get the sentence he deserves.'

'I'm more than happy to testify,' Georgina said. 'If you need a copy of the vet reports, let me know.' She looked at him. 'But I'd like to see him.'

'He's in London, in custody, on remand,' Colin said.

'Can you get me a visiting order? If you're worried about what I just said, I'm hardly going to whip out a hockey stick and start battering him with all the prison guards as witnesses.'

'Obviously,' Colin said. He sighed. 'Will it actually help? Because I worry that he'll upset you even more.'

'I want him to face what he did,' Georgina said. 'And I want him to apologise for what he did to Bert, and to Valerie.'

'I'm not sure he's capable of feeling remorse,' Colin said. 'You won't get an apology – at least, not a sincere one.' He filled her in on what Mei had told him.

'Poor Louise,' Georgina said. 'That's not going to be an easy conversation for you.'

'No,' Colin said with another sigh. 'But Larissa's going to sit with the kids so at least they won't overhear anything before Louise is ready to explain it to them. And I think the people of Wenborough will rally round the family.'

'I agree,' Georgina said.

Louise opened the door to Mill Cottage; she looked drawn and pale, Colin thought. Not that he was surprised. Her life had turned into a nightmare.

'Detective Inspector Bradshaw and Detective Constable Foulkes.' She bit her lip. 'Is Annie not with you?'

'No,' he said gently. 'Mrs Wilkins, we need to have a chat. I don't think the children should overhear this particular conversation, so Larissa's going to sit with them while we talk in a different room.'

She nodded, and ushered them through to the kitchen, where the children were sitting at the table with a drink and a snack. Colin, sensing that Louise needed some time to bolster herself for even more bad news, accepted the offer of tea. Louise introduced Larissa to the children, suggested going to watch TV in the living room, and asked Sam to show Larissa the way.

'How bad is it?' Louise asked quietly when the children were out of earshot.

'It's grim,' Colin said, and filled her in on what Hugo and Annie had done.

By the time he'd finished, Louise was shaking. 'I don't know whether to cry, scream or smash every bit of crockery,' she said. 'Oh, my God. I know Hugo had a couple of affairs during our marriage and I turned a blind eye because – well, I didn't want the kids to have a weekend dad. But that's what he was becoming anyway. And to have a fling with our nanny...' She shook her head. 'That's wrong on so many levels. It's too close to home, not to mention taking advantage of someone younger than him, someone who's vulnerable. It's like middle-aged men hitting on young bar staff in the pub because they know the girls would be too scared of losing their jobs to complain. I could *punch* him for that. And making half the village sick and killing poor Mrs Waring, just because he wasn't getting his own way, putting his own kids at risk, doing his best to ruin my business – I hope you throw the book at him and he stays behind bars for years and years and years. I want a divorce.' She blew out a breath. 'And poor Marion. What a horrible way to die. It's horrible to think that if Georgie hadn't warned me of her suspicions, I might have ended up dead, too. Even though Georgie got the wrong suspect, I'm glad I listened to her and didn't eat the chili.' Her eyes filled with tears. 'If I'd died, what would have happened to Sam, Noah and Isla?'

Unless someone else in the family had been able to take them in, Colin thought, they would have ended up in care, and possibly not together. Not that Louise needed the extra anguish of knowing that. 'I'm sorry to be the bearer of bad news,' he said. 'Do you have anyone who can support you?'

'My sister,' Louise said. 'She never liked Hugo. She said he was an entitled arse. And she was right. Part of me wishes I'd listened to her and never married him, but then again that would mean I didn't have Sam, Noah and Isla. They're the lights of my life. It's not their fault their dad's a scumbag.' She looked at Colin. 'What happens now?'

'They're both in custody – Hugo in London, and Annie in Norwich,' Colin said. 'We'll put the cases to the Crown Prosecution Service, who will decide whether they want to press charges. But we have signed confessions from both of them, along with evidence to show what happened, so there's a high chance of conviction. I think it'll be a matter of waiting for a court date.'

'Are they likely to go to jail?'

'Yes,' Colin said. 'Unless there are mitigating circumstances.'

'No. There aren't any,' Louise said. 'I'll parcel Annie's things up and send them back to her parents. And Hugo's stuff can go to his brother or to the tip.' She grimaced. 'I don't care which. But I swear he's never setting foot in this house again.'

Georgina hugged Will. 'I'm sorry this didn't turn out to be the nice relaxing week at home that it was supposed to be, love.'

He hugged her back. 'It certainly took my mind off my problems. I thought I was going to help you solve a cold case, and instead it turned out to be murder at the windmill. I'm just glad *you're* all right.'

'Have you thought about what you're going to do?' she asked.

He nodded. 'I've already applied for a few jobs and spoken to some dedicated scientific recruitment agents. And because I know I don't have to put up with Jill for much longer – I'm pretty sure when I hand in my notice in, they'll put me on garden leave – I can cope with her.'

'Good,' Georgina said. 'Let me know you get home safely.'

'I will,' he promised. 'And keep me posted if you get any responses from those social media posts about Margaret Chorley.'

SIXTEEN

TWO MONTHS LATER

The daffodils were out, the sky was a promising spring blue, and the world was looking brighter in Little Wenborough. Georgina went to two court dates with Louise Wilkins, while Jodie agreed to collect Louise's children from school and nursery and give them their dinner if Louise and Georgina weren't back in time.

Annie Newman was found guilty of the murder of Marion Wilkins and Miss Hurst, and Hugo Wilkins was found guilty of the manslaughter of Valerie Waring, plus causing unnecessary suffering to Bert.

As Colin had predicted, the residents of Great and Little Wenborough rallied round Louise and her children, and one of Jodie's friends became Louise's new childminder.

And Georgina came home to an unexpected message in response to her social media posts.

Dear Georgina – I hope I may call you that? My grandson saw your post about Margaret Chorley, and he recognised the name of the grocer from Bawburgh who allegedly sold her the poison that killed Daniel Forrest. That was my great-grandfather, John Sayers. My grandfather didn't want to take over the business, so John sold up. Before he died, as an old man, he confessed to my father – his grandson – that as a young man he'd done something very wrong. He'd lied in court.

He told the judge that he'd sold poison to a young woman, when he'd done nothing of the kind. She always bought arsenic to control the rats at her windmill from the chemist in her own village. But he was persuaded to lie and to suggest that she'd bought the arsenic from him to evade suspicion from her regular supplier.

The man who persuaded him to lie was an unpleasant man called Herbert Forrest. He was a corn factor – a dealer – who also owned several mills in the area. Margaret Chorley was taking over the running of the mill from her father and Forrest wanted the business. He knew the only way to get his hands on the mill would be if he could somehow get her out of the way. Forrest also owned various other businesses and properties, including the shop my great-grandfather leased. He told my great-grandfather that if he wanted to keep the lease, he'd have to do Forrest a favour and lie for him in court. If he didn't, the lease would be terminated and Forrest would tell everyone how unreliable he was.

My grandfather and his twin brother had just been born. John Sayer couldn't afford to be out of work with no prospects, not with two new babies. He didn't want them all ending up in the workhouse. He desperately needed to keep the lease. So he said in court exactly what Forrest wanted him to say – and the lie haunted him for the rest of his days. When Margaret was found guilty of the murder, he was horrified and he knew his testimony had sent an innocent woman to the gallows. But changing his plea would mean admitting the perjury in the first place, which he knew would get him into trouble, and it would also mean that Forrest would terminate the lease and his family would end up on the streets. My great-uncle was poorly at the time and John needed every penny to pay the doctor.

At the end of his life, he finally told the truth via my father and asked the vicar for absolution. My father wrote everything down in his diary, and I'm very happy to let you have a copy as part of your case to overturn this miscarriage of justice.

Kind regards
Kelsey Sayers

'So now we know what happened,' Georgina said to Colin. 'Poor Margaret.'

'But now you've cleared her name and you can make sure the truth is known,' Colin reminded her.

Over the next couple of months, the village history society supported Georgina and Louise in putting together the case for Parliament to issue a posthumous pardon for Margaret Chorley. Her diary – the one she'd been looking for at the mill – went to the county records office; the village put a small memorial stone and a rose bush in the churchyard; and Louise put together a display board at the mill, telling Margaret's story.

'Margaret says thank you,' Doris reported. 'At long last she's going to be reunited with her father – and at long last she'll be at peace.'

'Good. Though it's a shame that Forrest is never going to have to face up to what he did,' Georgina said.

'He'll be remembered for what he was – a liar and a cheat, and most likely the one who poisoned the flour,' Doris said. 'Which is the best outcome we could have achieved.'

'Team Little Wenborough,' Georgina said with a smile.

'I'll raise a cup of tea to that,' Doris said. 'Though I have a feeling that's not going to be our last case...'

A LETTER FROM THE AUTHOR

Huge thanks for reading *The Body at the Windmill*; I hope you enjoyed Georgina, Doris and Colin's journey. If you want to join other readers in hearing all about my new releases and bonus content, you can sign up for my newsletter.

www.stormpublishing.co/kate-hardy

If you enjoyed this book and could spare a few moments to leave a review, that would be hugely appreciated. Even a short review can make all the difference in encouraging a reader to discover my books for the first time. Thank you so much!

This series was hugely influenced by three things. Firstly, I grew up in a haunted house in a small market town in Norfolk, so I've always been drawn to slightly spooky stories. (I did research it when I wrote a book on researching house history, but I couldn't find any documentary evidence for the tale of the jealous miller who murdered his wife. However, I also don't have explanations for various spooky things that happened at the house – including the anecdote about Sybbie's dogs in *The Body at Rookery Barn*, which happened in real life with our Labradors and a tennis ball.) Secondly, I read Daphne du Maurier's short story 'The Blue Lenses' while I was a student, and... I can't explain this properly without giving spoilers, so I'll say it's to do with how you see people. Thirdly, I'm deaf; after I had my first hearing aid fitted, once I'd got over the thrill of hearing birdsong for the first time in years, my author brain started ticking. The du Maurier story gave me a 'what if' moment: what if you heard something through your hearing aids that wasn't what you were supposed to hear? (The obvious one would be someone's thoughts; but that's where my childhood home came in.) It took a few years for the idea to come to the top of my head and refuse to go away, but what if you could hear what my heroine Georgina ends up hearing?

And so Georgina Drake ends up living in a haunted house in a small market town in Norfolk...

The Body at the Windmill owes a big nod to the house where I grew up (though our windmill was dismantled about a century before we moved there), and Georgina's delight in the nerdy documents and books during her research pretty much mirrors my own. In the course of writing local history books, I've fossicked in the archives at the Forum library in Norwich, and worked with original murder broadsides as well as microfiche (and original!) copies of the local paper. I also happen to own a couple of very old trade directories, which I enjoyed using to inspire details for my fictional villages. As part of my research, I also visited various windmills in Norfolk (and sent my research assistant – aka my husband – up to the top of one of them to take photos, when I wussed out because the final ladder was a bit *too* steep and narrow for my liking). A lot of windmills across the country are open during National Windmill Day in May, and it's fascinating to see how everything works.

The cold case was inspired in part by a couple of local cases (including John Stratford, the Dumpling Poisoner – that's where the arsenic in the flour comes from), and Will's comments about Victorian murders and the uses of arsenic are all based on real-life cases from the 1800s. Norwich Castle was indeed the county prison in the nineteenth century, and the executions took place on the bridge by the gatehouse towers. The printer Robert Walker was a real person, based in Coslany, who published several of the murder broadsides; although the broadside in this book is fictional, the real-life ones have the same format of a woodcut, a sensational tale and a moral ballad. Mackie's *Annals* is also real, and utterly fascinating; although I've worked with the original two-volume set, a digital copy is available online nowadays as part of Project

Gutenberg. Quite a lot of old local newspapers across the country have also been digitised, and some are available free to access at the British Newspaper Archive as part of the British Library's digitisation project; others are available via a genealogy website subscription (although some library services offer free access to readers on computers at their branches).

Little Wenborough isn't a real place, but the name is a mashup of the town where I grew up and the river where I walk my dogs in the morning. Several of the places I mention are real, and I'd definitely recommend a visit to both Blickling Hall and Foxley Wood for the bluebells. Norfolk is an amazing place to live. Huge skies (with incredible sunrises and sunsets), wide beaches (aka my best place to think, and the Editpawial Assistants are always up for a trip to Wells-next-the-Sea), and more ancient churches than anywhere else in the country (watch this space for the next book in the series...).

Thanks again for being part of this amazing journey with me and I hope you'll stay in touch – I have so many more stories and ideas to entertain you with!

All best,

Kate Hardy

ACKNOWLEDGMENTS

I'd like to thank Oliver Rhodes and Kathryn Taussig for taking a chance on my slightly unusual take on a crime series; Emily Gowers for being an absolute dream of an editor – incisive, thoughtful and a wonderful collaborator as well as being great fun; and Shirley Khan and Maddy Newquist for picking up the bits I missed! I've loved every second of working on this book with you.

Gerard has been a particular star with location research on this book (aka 'Are you sure this windmill exists and we can actually go inside it?').

Special thanks to my family and friends who cheer-led the first Georgina Drake book, made useful suggestions about wind-mills/cake for this one, and are there through the highs and lows of publishing. You know who you are, and I appreciate you all.

Extra-special thanks to Gerard, Chris and Chloë Brooks, who've always been my greatest supporters; to Chrissy and Rich Camp, for always believing in me and being the best uncle and aunt ever; and to Archie and Dexter, my beloved Editpawial Assis-tants, for keeping my feet warm, reminding me when it's time for walkies and lunch and putting up with me photographing them to keep my social media ticking over while I'm on deadline.

And, last but very much not least, thank *you*, dear reader, for choosing my book. I hope you enjoy reading it as much as I enjoyed writing it.